To Dance
at the Palais Royale

Janet McNaughton

Stoddart Kids
TORONTO • NEW YORK

The author acknowledges the kind assistance of the Cooperation
Agreement on Cultural Industries in funding research related to this
book, and the Canada/Newfoundland Agreement on Economic
Renewal for advertising, tour, publicity and promotion assistance.

*We acknowledge the Canada Council for the Arts and the
Ontario Arts Council for their support of our publishing program.*

First published in 1996 by
Tuckamore Books a Creative Publishers imprint
P.O. Box 8660, St. John's Newfoundland A1B 3T6

Published in Canada in 1998 by
Stoddart Kids,
a division of Stoddart Publishing Co. Limited
34 Lesmill Road
Toronto, Canada M3B 2T6
Tel (416) 445-3333 Fax (416) 445-5967
E-mail Customer.Service@ccmailgw.genpub.com

Published in the United States in 1999 by
Stoddart Kids,
a division of Stoddart Publishing Co. Limited
180 Varick Street, 9th Floor
New York, New York 14207
Toll free 1-800-805-1083
E-mail gdsinc@genpub.com

Distributed in Canada by
General Distribution Services
325 Humber College Blvd.
Toronto, Canada M9W 7C3
Tel (416) 213-1919 Fax (416) 213-1917
E-mail Customer.Service@ccmailgw.genpub.com

Distributed in the United States by
General Distribution Services
85 River Rock Drive, Suite 202
Buffalo, New York 14207
Toll free 1-800-805-1083
E-mail gdsinc@genpub.com

Canadian Cataloguing in Publication Data

McNaughton, Janet Elizabeth, 1953–
To dance at the Palais Royale

ISBN 0-7736-7473-X

I. Title.

PS8575.N385T6 1998   jC813'.54   C98-930492-2
PZ7.M35To 1998

Cover art: Jennifer Pohl
Cover design: Tannice Goddard
Printed and bound in Canada

Dedication

For my daughter, Elizabeth Wallack:

So you will know what happened before you were here, my love.

Table of Contents

Acknowledgments

Writing is not necessarily a lonely occupation. As Writers in Residence at Memorial University, Kevin Major and Marilyn Bowering read early drafts of this work and provided helpful insights. I also thank members of the Newfoundland Writers' Guild, Gordon Rodger's Work-in-Progress workshop at the Writers' Alliance of Newfoundland and Labrador AGM in 1994, and Carmelita McGrath's Advanced Fiction Writing course offered by Continuing Studies at Memorial University — especially Gordon, Carmelita, Libby Creelman, and Shree Ghatage. I thank Peter Carver for his editorial skill, and my publisher Don Morgan, who brooks my considerable interference with remarkable tolerance.

The Federal-Provincial Cooperation Agreement on Cultural Industries gave me a grant to visit Toronto in 1995. During that time and after, I received valuable assistance from staff at the City of Toronto Archives, the Metro Toronto Central Reference Library, the Metro Urban Affairs Library, the Deer Park Public Library, the Toronto Harbour Commission Archives, and the Ontario Jewish Archives. Thanks especially to Michele Dale and Dr. Stephen Speisman from those last two respectively. Closer to home, I must thank the Folklore and Language Archive, Memorial University of Newfoundland (as always) and the Centre for Newfoundland Studies — especially its wonderful director, Anne Hart, who also read a draft of the novel and provided factual help and kind support. A conversation with Ken Oppel on the state of YA literature inadvertently led me to the title of this book.

My mother's extended family shared their memories with me for most of my childhood, and in a more formal way in 1977, when I interviewed them about coming to Canada.

My mother Isabel McNaughton, her sisters Jean Shepherd, Barbara McCormack, and Janet Young, and her brother Joe McIvor, all helped me more than I can say. My Aunt Jean and Uncle Joe have died since then. I hope this book would have pleased them.

"My Love is Like a Red, Red Rose" is by Robert Burns. "She's Like a Swallow" is a Newfoundland folksong, collected by Maud Karples in 1929. The lyrics reproduced here are from the author's memory. The poem, "The Sick Rose," by William Blake, is from *Songs of Experience*. I first read the folktale about the jar of tears in *Canadians of Old* by Philippe Aubert de Gaspé, translated by Charles G.D. Roberts. The story of the domestic who shot her employer and was acquitted is taken from Genevieve Leslie's "Domestic Service in Canada, 1880-1920," in *Women at Work, 1850-1930*. Also useful were Ruth Frager's *Sweatshop Strife: Class, Ethnicity and Gender in the Jewish Labour Movement of Toronto, 1900-1939*, Stephen Speisman's *The Jews Of Toronto: A History to 1937*, and Ronald Noseworthy's 1971 unpublished MA thesis, "A Dialect Survey of Grand Bank, Newfoundland."

Finally, I thank my husband Michael because he never reads a word I write and is (almost) always on my side.

Dougie

Aggie sat by the fire, warming her feet on the fender. It was night and the room was filled with orange light and flickering shadows. The house was never empty, and yet it was empty now. But Aggie didn't wonder why, for suddenly there was her brother Dougie, dressed in his pit clothes, home for the day, laughing as he always did.

Somewhere in Aggie's mind a memory sparked. Wasn't Dougie dead? She quickly smothered the thought. How could Dougie be dead? Here he was, tall and handsome, even with the coal dust streaking his face. But the sadness that was never far from the surface welled up in Aggie now as she looked at Dougie, and she began to cry. He came to her.

"Aggie," he said, "what's wrong?"

"Oh Dougie," she said through her tears, "I'll be going to Canada soon. How can I leave you?"

He laid his blackened hand against her cheek. "You know it's right to go, Aggie. The money will be a great help to Mum and Da. I'm past worrying about now."

And Aggie realized that even though Dougie was with her, he was dead. She stood and put her head on his shoulder and cried and cried. But the tears were a comfort; they eased her pain.

Chapter One

Loughlinter

When she opened her eyes every morning, she saw four panes of glass. Not the view beyond them, but the glass itself, coated with fine coal dust. So much coal dust that it was easy to forget what a window was for. Through the window, through the coal dust, the lights of the pit head shone in the early morning darkness. But Aggie could only see them when she remembered to look.

Aggie always woke early, when the house was dark and still. This was the best time of day to remember dreams and ponder the future. She strained now to see the lights of the pit head, where the men of Loughlinter, her father among them, went underground each day to hack coal from the wet, black mine. Her brother Dougie had died not a year ago because of that mine. Dougie. The sight of the pit head brought her dream back to her.

It was not the sadness she remembered now, but the comfort, the feeling of having Dougie near again. Aggie snuggled against her youngest sister under the warm covers. Less than two weeks, she thought, only twelve more days. Then I leave for Canada. Aggie looked at her younger sisters sleeping near. Little Jen was curled into a tight ball beside

Aggie, her dark blond hair spilling over the pillow. Jen was Aggie's special pet. Across the room in the other bed, Flora was buried under the covers so only her nose poked out. At fourteen, Flora had already left school and was working as a domestic servant. The three boys, Ewan, James, and Callum, had their own room across the hall.

Aggie slipped out of bed without waking Jen and dressed quietly. She went downstairs and lit the fire and made a pot of tea before her mother even stirred. The bare kitchen with its few sticks of furniture reminded Aggie that her mother's life had been hard enough, raising eight children on so little money. Her father's wages were decided by the amount of coal he mined, not the hours he worked. He always handed the money over to his wife on payday, never stopping to drink it away as some men did. But when the coal wasn't there, his pay was small.

When her mother came downstairs and found the tea waiting a few minutes later, she smiled.

"Aggie, you're as handy as a wee teapot." Aggie flushed with pride. Not many words were wasted on praise in this house.

As Aggie ate, her mother sat across the table with a cup of tea.

"We'll let Flora sleep a wee bit more," she said. Aggie could see that her mother took pleasure in this rare moment of rest and quiet. But she ate without meeting her mother's eyes. Lately, Aggie noticed something different in the way her mother looked at her, something that made it hard for Aggie to breathe.

At first Aggie had not known what that look meant. Now she recalled how she'd understood. A few weeks ago, Flora had come home talking excitedly about Canada. Any scrap of news about Canada was carefully hoarded, examined, and discussed, like her sister Emma's letters from Toronto, which were read and re-read until the paper went limp and tore at the creases.

"Mrs. MacCluskie said her cousin had a letter from her daughter in Toronto," Flora had announced. "She said the people in Toronto are so rich, they heat the streets in wintertime."

"Heat the streets? That canna be true," their father had said. Douglas Maxwell was a man who took nothing at face value.

"Oh aye, Da, it is," insisted Flora. "She said you can see steam rising through grates in the streets everywhere."

A lively debate followed on the likelihood of heated streets, all the children clamouring to be heard.

"Well, Aggie," Douglas Maxwell said finally, turning to her, "when you get to Toronto, that's your first task. Find out if they really heat the streets, and write back to us." Everyone had laughed, but by chance Aggie had glanced around to see her mother quickly wipe her eyes on the hem of her apron. Aggie looked away, but the pain she felt almost made her catch her breath. She knew then what was in her mother's look — it was longing. With Dougie dead and Emma gone to Canada, her mother seemed to miss her already.

"Will you see Davy tonight?" her mother asked. Aggie came abruptly back to the present. Before Dougie died, Davy had been his closest friend. He often called for Aggie now although they were not really courting — could not be since Aggie was leaving so soon.

"Well, he often waits outside Mrs. MacDougall's to walk me home." Aggie found herself blushing. "I plan to take the wee ones out when I get home this aft, Mum. Davy can come with us if he wants to," she said. She gathered up her dishes without meeting her eyes mother's eyes, kissing the top of her head as she passed on the way to the dish basin. "If I'm no careful I'll be late." It was a good excuse to end the conversation.

The February wind blew damp and raw as Aggie made her way to the MacDougall house. She knew she had been lucky to find a place with Mrs. MacDougall, an old widow, rich by Loughlinter standards. She had a live-in housekeeper, a hired washerwoman, and kept Aggie just for daily housework, and perhaps because she brightened the place.

Aggie was glad to come into Mrs. MacDougall's warm, bright kitchen where Ritchie, the housekeeper, held sway. It should have been Mrs. Ritchie, but no one called her that. She was stout and jolly and kind, full of laughter and gossip, so different from most Loughlinter folk that she was not well liked outside the house where she worked.

"Even a fool looks like a wise man if he keeps his mouth shut." That was what they said in Loughlinter. But Ritchie never held her tongue, never kept her opinions to herself. Mrs. MacDougall enjoyed that. At first, Aggie was shocked by both old ladies. Surely there must be something sinful about enjoying life as much as they did, trying recipes just for fun, playing music on the Victrola (even on a Sunday!), playing cards — something strictly forbidden in most Loughlinter households. But both women were so kindly, so well-meaning in spite of their gossip, that Aggie grew to love them, and her working days, which should have been dreary, were a patch of brightness in the grey world of Loughlinter.

"Ah, there you are, pet," cried Ritchie now. "Just in time to take the missus her breakfast." And a tray of hot tea, fresh scones, and kippers under a covered dish was placed in her arms as soon as her coat was off. The smell of the kippers tickled Aggie's nose, reminding her of her own meagre breakfast, a bowl of oatmeal small enough to be sure that the children would not go hungry.

A bright blaze was already burning in the fireplace of Mrs. MacDougall's bedroom. The old lady was sitting up in bed with a shawl around her shoulders, her hairnet still in place.

"Ah, there you are, Aggie, hen," she said as the door opened. "What will I do without you?" Then, removing the cover from the dish she exclaimed. "Och. Ritchie made too many kippers for an old soul like me. Here, hen, take one, you're too thin in any case." And the "extra" kipper was put on an extra plate that had somehow also found its way onto the tray. Aggie couldn't tell which of the old ladies, Ritchie or Mrs. MacDougall or both, had engineered that kipper onto that tray, but she knew it was no accident and ate in grateful silence.

Her days at the MacDougall house passed like this, full of laughter and pleasant surprises. Not that she didn't work. Out of gratitude, she made the house shine. This day flew by like all the others and soon it was time to go home.

Aggie knew that Davy would be waiting for her when she stepped into the damp night air, and so he was. He slouched against the lamp post, his cloth cap pulled low on his brow, his hands, now permanently stained with coal dust no matter how he washed them, thrust down in his pants' pockets. He grinned when he caught sight of her. She was never really sure how she felt about Davy, but that grin always made her smile. With his golden brown hair and laughing blue eyes, he was so handsome that any girl would be proud to be seen with him, although in truth he seemed never to notice his looks. Of course she was fond of him because he had been Dougie's friend. But she knew Davy hoped for something more.

Aggie had no clear idea what something more might mean. She knew about hugging and kissing, but little else. New babies appeared frequently in the Maxwell household with never a word to explain where they might have come from. Had Aggie been bold enough to ask, her questions would have met a shocked silence. In any case, Davy was always a gentleman, and never did more than take her arm at the elbow when they walked. And she was glad of that, because she wasn't ready for more.

By rights, she knew, she shouldn't let Davy wait for her like this, or sit with her in church, or take her to the cinema to see the picture shows as he sometimes did. This was court-ing, and that was not fair to him since she would soon be gone. Perhaps she was leading him on by letting him do these things, and Emma said that leading a lad on was a terrible sin. But she enjoyed Davy's company, and she didn't feel she was doing wrong.

"So, lass," he said now, "what are your plans for the evening?"

"I told my mum I'd take the wee ones out for a while — just down the glen, I thought."

"Do you want me to come with you, then?" Davy asked. "To keep those wee heathens from running wild?"

"I canna stop you, Davy, if that's your wish." And that was her way of saying yes.

It was Dougie who had first drawn Davy into Aggie's family, but now he seemed to like all the Maxwells, even the noisy younger children. Aggie knew other girls in Loughlin-ter wished they were in her place. Even the ones who worked in shops, girls who normally thought themselves too good to be seen with miners, made a point of speaking to Davy. But, for reasons Aggie didn't understand, she was the one he had chosen.

The younger children, all four of them, had been told by their mother to expect an outing when Aggie got home, and they met her with excited whoops. They seemed to be everywhere at once.

"Och, Aggie's brought her lad home!" little Callum cried. "Did you bring us any sweeties, then?" he demanded.

"Whist you, Callum," said their mother, "or you'll stay here while the others go." And she smiled an apology at Davy. There were really too many children for her to teach proper manners to now, especially with the older ones gone.

The children swarmed over the house, picking up hats and coats, looking for stray shoes, until at last all were ready to leave —even Jen, the youngest, who had somehow lost a shoe and cried loudly for fear she would be left behind. The children spilled outside and ran down the narrow, cobblestone streets, shouting as they ran. Aggie and Davy followed.

A few blocks from the Maxwell house, Loughlinter gave way to a rocky glen with small farms beyond. The children plunged down the steep side of the glen, yelling back and forth, looking for early spring flowers. Davy sat with Aggie on a rock. Once he reached out on impulse to take Aggie's hand, but she startled at his touch, pulling away quickly. He did not try again.

It was dark before the children had run themselves out. Aggie and Davy herded them home.

"Goodbye, Aggie," Davy said on the doorstep. "I'll be in church on Sunday." She only nodded, but they both knew they had just agreed to meet there.

Jane Maxwell welcomed her children home, rising from the fireside where she had been sitting alone, mending the younger ones' clothes. When Aggie thought of her mother, she pictured her just like this, bent over her mending in the dim firelight, repairing clothes into the night so the little ones would have something to wear the next day. Aggie's father was not home. He spent all his spare time just outside of Loughlinter, tending the pigeons he raised with his brother.

Now their mother shooed the young ones upstairs, leaving Flora to get them ready for bed while Aggie ate her supper. Aggie suspected her mother had planned this with Flora so she could spend some time alone with her. The thumps, giggles, and squeals of the younger children sounded above their heads as Aggie ate.

"I had a letter from Em today," her mother said. "She's looking forward to seeing you." Aggie nodded wordlessly. It was not always a comfort to think that her older sister was waiting on the other side of the ocean. After Dougie died, Emma, who was dark and wilful and pretty, had hatched the scheme that would bring the whole family to Canada. Emma had learned about the reduced passage program. The Canadian government covered most of the expenses for young British girls if they came to Canada to work as domestic servants. It cost next to nothing and there were plenty of jobs, because Canadian girls wouldn't work as servants.

At nineteen, Emma was fearless and bored with Loughlinter. She'd argued and pleaded, bribing the little ones with sweets, boldly asking her parents if they wanted all their sons dead of the mines, until everyone had agreed to her plan. Last fall she had sailed for Canada and taken a position in a house in Toronto. Now it was Aggie's turn. You had to be seventeen to make the trip. Aggie would sail on her seventeenth birthday: February 15, 1928. All the money she and Emma could spare would be sent home, and if everything went well the rest of the family would come to Canada in a few years. None of her younger brothers would ever go into the mines.

But Emma was the only one of her brothers and sisters that Aggie ever argued with. And Aggie was happy in

Loughlinter. Sometimes, just thinking about leaving gave Aggie a lump in her throat. Tonight, her mother seemed to notice. She sat down, putting her hand over Aggie's. Aggie kept her eyes down, looking at her mother's hands. Once, they had been beautiful. The fingers were still long and delicate, but now the skin was work-roughened and her nails were cracked and split.

"Aggie," she said, "I know this is harder for you than it was for Em. No one she worked for was ever as kind to her as Mrs. MacDougall and Ritchie are to you. And Emma wouldn'a have any of the lads who were always coming round for her. I knew she'd find her way out of Loughlinter, but I didn'a think she'd take us all with her. And I know it must be hard for you to leave Davy."

Her mother paused. Aggie felt herself blush. Everyone was certain, if she stayed, that Davy would eventually ask her to marry him. But her mother never spoke of this. No one did. She hoped, if she said nothing now, her mother might stop. But she went on.

"Aggie, if you were to stay in Loughlinter, I know what would happen to you, lass. You'd marry Davy, just as I married your Da, all full of hope. But every year would bring another baby, and soon there'd be too many mouths to feed. No matter how hard Davy worked, there would never be enough money or enough food. I want you to understand, lass. This isn'a just for the boys' sake. You and Emma and Flora and Jen will have a better life away from the mines too."

There were tears in her mother's eyes now. Aggie knew if she tried to speak she would cry too. So she only nodded. Her mother patted her hand, then rose from the table and took up her mending by the fire again.

Chapter Two

The Collection Basket

"Aggie, I canna find my braces."

Aggie sighed. Callum's suit was bulky and ill-fitting, an old one of Dougie's, cut down. The pants would never stay up without braces. And Callum's braces were always missing on a Sunday morning. Aggie never knew whether they disappeared because Callum was so careless, or if this was his way of trying to avoid church. She found the braces under Callum's bed. Flora rounded up the others. Finally, everyone was gathered in the kitchen.

"Are we ready then?" Aggie asked.

"I dinna want to go, Aggie. Could I no stay home? Please? I'll be good." It was Jen, the youngest. Aggie knew why she asked. Their brothers wriggled and squirmed and tried to make Jen cry out or giggle, bringing stern looks from the adults in the congregation.

Their mother spoke from the basin where she washed the breakfast dishes.

"Aggie, I wonder why you bother. Taking this lot to church is like taking a pack of puppies, and about as much good. They never listen."

Aggie looked down at her smallest sister's worried face. Even strangers sometimes commented on the resemblance between Jen and Aggie. They both had the same thick hair, small, sharp faces, and large, grey eyes. Aggie would not usually try to take all the wee ones to church, but as the time to leave approached she found herself wanting to spend more time with them. Especially Jen. And Aggie knew their mother needed some rest and quiet. She leaned over and cuddled the younger girl.

"Jen, please, will you no do this just for me?"

The child gave a sigh that seemed too big for her small, thin frame and said, "If you ask me like that, I canna say no."

Aggie laughed.

Davy met them just inside the church. Usually, they sat on either side of the children to keep order. But today Davy let the children go past him and sat by Aggie's side. She knew this was probably asking for trouble, but it seemed heartless to ask him to move.

This Sunday there was a special collection for the church missions in China and Aggie had scraped together a few extra ha'pennies for her brothers and sisters. The children never saw money. Aggie saw the longing in their faces as she passed the coins to them.

The grey stone church was unheated, the minister old, and his sermons dull. The children had reason to misbehave. At least this week the hymns were lively. Before the mission collection they sang "Bringing In the Sheaves." Jen, who knew all the words, sang with fervour. Aggie and Davy shared a single hymn book, standing close together. Aggie worried about gossip. Then she realized it didn't matter — she would soon leave all gossip behind.

The collection baskets were passed along on long poles. They were made of wicker and emptied from the bottom by a hinge. Aggie was busy putting all the hymn books back when the basket passed along her pew. Davy was busy watching her.

And that was how they failed to see what happened.

Later, at noon dinner Aggie noticed something was wrong.

"Jen," she said, "are you ill? You've barely touched your food." The child nodded miserably. "She didn'a want to go to church this morning either," Aggie recalled.

"Come here, pet, and let me feel your head," their mother said. Jen did. "Well, there's no fever. Do you want to lie down, Jen?"

Jen nodded. Aggie took her upstairs while the table was cleared.

"Just rest a wee while," Aggie said as she tucked a blanket around her and kissed her forehead. "I'm sure you'll feel better soon." Jen nodded, turned her face to the wall, and closed her eyes. She must be sick, Aggie thought. Jen never slept during the day.

Aggie was busy washing the dishes when Callum crept upstairs to Jen's bedroom. If anyone had noticed, they might have wondered at his unusual concern for his sister's health.

Jen seemed well enough to go to school the next morning, but at supper Aggie thought she still seemed subdued. Remembering Dougie's illness, which had come on gradually at first, Aggie decided to keep an eye on Jen. In only a little more than a week Aggie would be on the boat to Canada. The thought of Jen falling ill now was more than she could bear. Every night at bedtime, Aggie checked to see if Jen looked pale or felt hot. Every night, there were no obvious signs of illness. Aggie only noticed that Jen was still strangely quiet and that she seemed....sticky.

Sticky was the only word. Jen's hands stuck to everything and were covered with fuzz from her woollen sweater, no matter how often Aggie sponged her clean. She also had a curious, sweet smell, something like peppermint. What kind of illness, Aggie wondered, could make a child smell like that? Then she noticed the boys were all the same — sticky and sweet-smelling. Aggie wondered if they had all fallen prey to the same rare disease. She said nothing to her mother for fear of worrying her.

But Aggie worried almost constantly as she went about her work at Mrs. MacDougall's. On Wednesday, Aggie was busy stocking the pantry with the week's grocery order when Mrs. MacDougall returned from a funeral. Aggie couldn't help overhearing the two older women as they gossiped in the kitchen.

"Well, we had a green Christmas. You know what folk say: a green Christmas means a full kirkyard," Ritchie said as she poured hot water into the teapot.

"Aye, that's so. But Lydia Thorburn was ailing for years. It was the strangest thing, though," Mrs. MacDougall said. "They said, before she died, she smelled like violets, sweet violets, just like perfume."

"Sometimes they say that those who've led good lives smell sweet before they die," Ritchie said. "I had an aunt..."

Thud! Both women to look up, startled. The sack of flour Aggie had been carrying was at her feet.

"Why Aggie, hen, are you ill? You're as white as a ghost. Sit down," Mrs. MacDougall cried, and both she and Ritchie eased Aggie into a chair and made her drink a cup of tea before she went back to work.

Those who've led good lives... Aggie went over the words in her mind again and again. The four wee ones, Jen and the boys, were certainly no better than other children. In fact, it seemed to Aggie they were in trouble more often than she and Dougie and Emma or even Flora had been when they were the same ages. But, over the last few days, ever since Sunday in fact, Jen did seem quieter and more thoughtful than usual. That night, at bedtime, as Aggie pulled a nightgown over Jen's temporarily unsticky hands and face, Jen said, "Aggie, do you think God gives things to people?"

"Well," Aggie said, "some things certainly. Mum and Da and all of us were given to one another by God."

Jen was not satisfied.

"I didn'a mean family. What about *things*?" She paused. "Money and the like."

"Well, I suppose some people might say so. Emma found out about Canada and went over there to earn more money for all of us, so we can get the boys away from the mines — maybe God helped her."

"That isn'a quite what I meant," Jen said. But when Aggie questioned her further, she yawned and said she was tired. As Aggie watched her fall asleep, the faint odour of peppermint filled the air.

Thursday afternoon was always maids' half day off. This was Aggie's last Thursday in Loughlinter and there was a great deal to do. Flora was left at home to make final preparations for the minister's tea. He would come to say goodbye to Aggie late in the afternoon. Before that, though, Aggie would finally see the Canadian doctor who travelled all over this part of Scotland giving medical exams. When he came to Loughlinter, the doctor used an empty room in the shipping agent's office. If Aggie failed this medical, she would not be allowed into Canada. After the medical, Aggie and her mother would finally pick up her steamship ticket. Before any of this, however, they were to visit Mr. Sheff, the old

Jewish tailor who could be trusted to lend money when it was needed.

Dressed in their best clothes, Aggie and her mother set out for Loughlinter's main streets — a few small shops crowded together on narrow, cobblestone roads. Everything, from the glass in the windows to the weathered paint on the woodwork, was covered in a fine rime of coal dust. Like most of Loughlinter, it looked old and tired.

Usually, Aggie's mother spoke only when words were needed. Now, she talked constantly as they walked along. Aggie could see something of her own nervousness reflected in her mother's chatter.

"Now you know how folk gossip, and I dinna doubt you've heard unpleasant things about Mr. Sheff, Aggie lass. Well, no one likes to be in debt. But if they need to borrow money and Mr. Sheff is willing to lend it, whose fault is that? He's a kind-hearted old soul. I know that myself. And there's more folk owe him money than you or I will ever know." She paused for a moment, then sighed. "I didn'a think I'd need to come to him again for you. Could we no save a few pounds? But Callum's shoes wore out, then Jen's blue dress — remember when it belonged to you? When I tried to mend it, it fell to pieces.

"But then Aggie, do you know, it's the strangest thing. When I picked up Callum's suit after church on Sunday what do you suppose I found? Half a crown in one of his pockets! Where could it have come from? Did you give the wee ones money for the collection on Sunday?"

"Yes, but only pennies, Mum. Where would any of us find half a crown?"

"That's just what I thought. I'm afraid we'll have to talk to him," she sighed. "I hope it's nothing. I'd hate to have to tell your Da."

Aggie knew why. There were some things Douglas Maxwell would not tolerate from his children, and stealing was one. It would certainly be bad for Callum if he had stolen the money. Callum was only eight, but he was the chief mischief-maker in the family. Aggie doubted that he would actually plan to steal, but if money came into his hands, he'd find it hard to return to its rightful owner. Her father was unbending in his ideas about honesty and that would count as stealing. Callum was certainly in trouble. Only one question remained in Aggie's mind. Why had he not spent the money as quickly as he could?

But there was no time to talk about this now, because they'd reached Mr. Sheff's shop. The bell above the door rang as they entered and Mr. Sheff came out from the back room. He had a small rimless cap on his head and wore a tailor's apron. He was an old man, thin and bent. His face lit up when he saw Aggie's mother.

"And so, Mrs. Maxwell, here is the next daughter," he said, smiling at Aggie. "Off she will go to Canada like her sister?"

"Yes, Mr. Sheff, with your kind help." Aggie could hear the embarrassment in her mother's voice.

The old man noticed and patted her hand.

"Well, it is a small thing I do, Mrs. Maxwell, and not everyone is thanking me." He turned to Aggie. "Your mother is kind to all peoples, not only her own. Most in this town have minds that are narrow. They see only what a person is, not into the heart. My sister went from Russia to Canada, to Montreal. In Canada, child, you will meet peoples from all lands. If you have the heart of your mother, you will do well." Then he drew a small green ledger from under the counter.

After the money changed hands, Aggie and her mother went to see the doctor. For the moment, Aggie's anxiety over the medical exam made her forget about Callum. She was sure there was nothing wrong with her, but it bothered her that she was still without her medical with the day of departure so near.

No one in Aggie's family ever saw a doctor unless something was very wrong. Dougie was dying the last time a doctor came to the Maxwell household. The prospect of seeing this doctor made Aggie remember Dougie's death. It had started with such a small accident, a blow to the chest from a stray shovel at the mine. But Dougie grew weaker and weaker, and in a few weeks he could no longer work. Then came the fever and his lapse into delirium.

Suddenly, her strong, healthy brother was slipping away from them, and nothing seemed to help. It was so much like a bad dream that Aggie had half believed she would wake up to find none of it was happening. Finally her mother had called the doctor, who came, listened to Dougie's chest, and said that he had pneumonia.

Aggie remembered one night especially. She had been sitting by the firelight in the kitchen where Dougie lay on a cot, bathed in sweat and mumbling senseless things. A knock had come at the door. When her mother answered, she found two old gypsy women —tinkers they were called. Like most of the town's people, Aggie feared the tinkers. They wore old clothes and had no real home and people said they stole little children away. But Jane Maxwell treated them with the same kindness she showed everyone, and they knew they could always find a place by her fire and a cup of tea.

These two women had not come for tea.

"We heard about your trouble, hen," they said to Jane. "We want to help." They told her they would make poultices from onions and place them around Dougie to drive the illness away.

When the doctor had learned of the plan he forbade it.

"If those tinkers come here with their home remedies, Mrs. Maxwell, I'll never set foot in this house again," he'd said. So, of course, nothing was done. Dougie died a few days later. He was twenty-one. Aggie still wondered if the tinkers could have saved him.

But this was a different doctor: the Canadian doctor. He was the first Canadian Aggie would ever meet. And he could keep her from going to Canada and ruin the family's plan. By the time they reached the shipping agent's office, Aggie had to force herself to take deep breaths. Two young women were just leaving when Aggie arrived with her mother. Aggie guessed they were domestics too. Aggie and her mother had just seated themselves in the small, dingy waiting room when a uniformed nurse came out and called, "Agnes Maxwell" in a crisp, highland accent.

The doctor was a big man, easily six feet tall, with sandy coloured hair and large, freckled hands. He seemed to fill the small office. He might have been a Canadian, but he looked just like anyone else. The nurse stood silently by. Aggie couldn't help staring at the large needle on the tray by her elbow.

"Maxwell," the doctor said as he checked her throat. "There was a girl named Maxwell through this office last fall, I believe. Any relation? Say 'ah' now."

It was difficult to follow the doctor's flat-sounding English at first. But after he looked in her throat Aggie found she understood.

"Oh, aye sir," she replied. "My sister."

"And now you want to come to Canada too, is that it?" he asked looking in her ears and eyes.

Before she remembered to be polite, Aggie found herself saying, "I dinna really want to, sir. It was my sister's idea."

And she explained the plan to get the boys away from the mines.

"Breathe in and out now while I listen to your chest," the doctor said when she finished. "Prospective immigrants are usually more eager to come to Canada than that." He laughed. "But don't worry, Agnes Maxwell. You may like it in spite of yourself."

"I'm going to Canada?"

"Certainly. You're perfectly healthy."

The doctor was about to pass Aggie on to the nurse for her vaccination when Aggie stopped him. She knew he was busy, but she wouldn't have a chance like this again. She took a deep breath and quickly said, "Doctor, I wonder, is there any illness a child of six could get that might make her smell...different?"

"How do you mean?"

"Well, sweet. Something like peppermint really." Aggie knew how silly this must sound. She felt her face burning. But the doctor seemed to take her seriously enough.

"Any other symptoms?"

"Well, she's been much quieter than usual and she's always sticky."

"Sticky?" The doctor laughed now. "Sounds like too much candy to me."

"Sweets? Oh, it couldn't'a be that. The wee ones never have money for..." Aggie remembered the half crown in Callum's pocket.

"Roll up your sleeve please, and I'll pass you along to the nurse. Don't worry. It doesn't sound serious to me."

When they returned home with the steamship ticket, there was just time to make the minister's tea. Flora had everything else ready, but she excused herself just before Mr.

Macleod arrived. He was a small, anxious old man, given to complaining and difficult to please.

They took Mr. Macleod into "the room" which was only used on very special occasions. "Well, Agnes," he said as he seated himself, "I've come to say my goodbyes to you. I suppose this sort of thing is necessary, but I canna say I think it wise. Mind you, I know a good girl like you will stay out of harm's way, but what's to become of most of these lassies, setting out alone for a strange land? I fear the worst for them. My Jane, this a fine treacle tart."

It was often said that Mr. Macleod could carry on a conversation in an empty room. He continued on now without stopping.

"I've my doubts about the moral fibre of this community even without all this immigration. Do you realize that someone robbed the collection basket in church last Sunday? Never, in all my years as a minister, have I encountered such a thing. It was when you had the wee ones to church with you, Agnes. A special collection for the missions in China too. I've not said a word about this to anyone to this very moment, hoping the culprit might repent. But it seems too late for that now."

Too late indeed, Aggie thought. Fortunately, the minister was busy with his plate. Aggie looked at her mother, who quickly erased the look of shock from her face.

"Another scone, Mr. Macleod?" Aggie's mother said hastily.

"Why, yes, Jane. Thank you." And he went on without noticing anything amiss.

Luckily, Mr. Macleod had another call to make and he was gone before the children returned from school. Aggie assembled Ewan, James, Callum, and Jen in the room. The children were unusually quiet. Except for special visitors, the room had not been used by the family since Dougie was laid out there before his burial. The children seemed to know what was going to happen. Aggie's mother ran her hands through her grey-streaked hair. She looked very old.

"Mr. Macleod told us about the collection basket," she said simply. "Tell us everything now, before your Da comes home. Callum, why did you steal the money?"

"I didn'a touch the collection basket," Callum said. "It was her." He pointed to Jen, who promptly burst into tears.

"He told me God wanted us to have the money," she sobbed, "because we never had money for sweets." She ran to Aggie and buried her face in her sister's lap. Her thin shoulders shook.

Aggie's mother was so surprised she couldn't speak. Aggie looked over Jen's head at Ewan, who was eleven.

"Tell us, Ewan, please."

"I didn'a see a thing, Aggie," he said.

"Da will be home soon." Even Aggie was surprised at the threatening note in her voice, but it worked.

"Well, I really didn'a see it happen," Ewan defended himself. "I only know what they told me. Just after the hymn, when the collection basket was passed, Callum pinched Jen."

Jen lifted her head from Aggie's lap and sniffed.

"It was a wicked pinch, Aggie. My knees flew up and hit the bottom of the collection basket."

Callum took up the story now.

"All the money dumped into her lap. She could have said something then, but she just took her hand and swung the basket shut. The money stayed in her lap."

"Who was taking the collection?" their mother asked. "Did he no see?"

"Tommy Stuart," Aggie recalled. "He never took his eyes off Jenny Morrison the whole time." Jenny was the church organist and Tommy's feelings for her were well known.

"But how did you hide the money, Jen?" their mother asked.

"I didn'a hide the money," Jen's voice broke. "Callum did."

"During the prayer," Ewan said. "When everyone's eyes were closed, Callum hid all the money in his suit pockets."

The big pockets, Aggie thought, of Dougie's old suit.

"I wanted to tell you, Aggie, honestly I did," Jen said. Then her voice dropped to a whisper. "I was so ashamed of myself."

"And that's why you seemed sick after the service?" Aggie asked.

Jen nodded.

"And then Callum came up to our room. He told me the money was a miracle, landing in my lap so quietly without anyone noticing. He said that God wanted us to have the money so we could buy sweets, because we're so poor."

Their mother looked at Callum, who scowled and said nothing. Then she turned to Ewan and James.

"When did you find out?" she asked. Her voice sounded very weary.

"Not until Monday at school," Ewan said.

"Did you no think to come to me?"

The two older boys looked uncomfortable.

"It seemed like telling," James said at last.

"And no doubt you had your share of sweets," their mother said. "If Flora was still at school, she might have saved your skins. Now, your Da will have to know."

Everyone knew what that meant.

When Douglas Maxwell came home from the mines that night he was told. After a painfully quiet supper which no one really ate, the children were ushered into the room again. This time Aggie and her mother stayed in the kitchen. Aggie strained to hear what her father was saying, but the words were lost. Only his tone, angry and hectoring, carried into the kitchen. There was a silence that seemed to last forever, then the sound of her father's belt hitting flesh and a cry of pain from one of the older boys.

Aggie rose quickly from the table where she had been toying with a cup of tea.

"I'm sorry, Mum, I canna stay." The words almost choked her as she fled up the stairs to her room. Flora was already there, sitting on her bed in the dark.

"Oh Aggie," she whispered, "I canna bear it." Aggie sat on the bed and slipped her arm around her sister's shoulder.

Little Jen was punished last, and, remembering how she had begged to stay home from church, each cry cut into Aggie's heart.

That night after Jen was finally settled, Aggie sat on the bed watching her little sister. Even in her sleep, Jen's small body still shook with sobs from time to time. The welts on her legs were horrible. Finally Jen seemed peaceful but Aggie was too upset to go to bed, so she went downstairs to find her mother. Aggie had assumed that her father would be gone to his pigeons. She would not have left the bedroom if she'd known she would meet him at the bottom of the stairs.

Even in the dim hall, she could see her father redden when he met her.

"You," he said, "are just as much to blame as the wee ones. Do you want them to grow up to be thieves? I expect you to take them to Mr. Macleod to make their apologies."

Aggie dropped her eyes and let her father pass. She was shaking when she went into the kitchen. Tears ran down her cheeks. Her mother had overheard.

"Dinna let him frighten you, lass," she said quietly. "He's only doing what he thinks best."

Aggie did not try to speak. Instead she put her head down on the kitchen table and sobbed. Her mother patted her shoulder sympathetically, but Aggie knew that her mother misunderstood. These were not tears of fear, but pure anger and frustration. What he did, Aggie thought, was wrong. It was wrong, and I'm too much of a coward to tell him so.

Aggie didn't miss Emma often, but she did now. If Emma were here she would have talked back. Aggie could see the spark in Emma's dark eyes, could imagine how she would stand up to their father. But Aggie didn't have the courage. She never had.

Most of the money from the church collection was already gone —spent on sweets for James and Ewan and Callum and Jen, and, Aggie and her mother discovered, virtually every other child at their school. It pleased Aggie to think they hadn't been miserly with the money, but she kept that thought to herself. The little money that remained was recovered, and Aggie brought the shame-faced children before the minister to explain themselves. Mr. Macleod was not nearly as angry as Aggie had expected.

"I suppose your father dealt with you?" he asked.

"Aye sir. He gave us a whipping with his belt," Ewan said.

"I'm pleased to hear that. You'll remember his lesson, I'm sure. Now, I'm in need of some helpers to mop the church floor each Saturday afternoon for the rest of the winter. That will help you remember not to steal as well." And that was all.

Aggie knew the whole episode was supposed to be forgotten after that. No one else gave it another thought, not even the children. But she couldn't get the sound of the children's cries, or the sight of the red welts on Jen's legs, out of her mind. In the short time left before she went to Canada, Aggie decided, she would avoid her father whenever she could.

Chapter Three

To Canada

Now time went by so quickly that Aggie felt like someone on a raft being drawn towards a waterfall, something she saw once at a picture show Davy had taken her to. Soon she would be over that waterfall, out on the ocean with no way back home.

Aggie was to work until the very day before she left. But Mrs. MacDougall and Ritchie let her do no work that day. Instead she was treated like a guest. At noon they sat with her at the big dining room table, and she shared the scotch broth and roast lamb, the turnip, peas, and potatoes, the tea and cakes prepared for her as if she were a Sunday guest. After the dishes were cleared away, the two old ladies looked at each other with mischief in their eyes. Aggie wondered what was next.

"Let's just go into the room, hen," Mrs. MacDougall said, "to sit a wee while." Aggie always loved this parlour with its dark papered walls, high bookshelves, and over-stuffed furniture. There, on the pump organ, was a big square parcel. After Aggie sat down, Ritchie brought it over to her.

"This is for you, pet. We couldn'a let you leave without some wee thing to remember us by."

Inside the box was a navy silk dress with a sailor collar, a drop waist, and a pleated skirt. It had white mother of pearl buttons and white satin piping for trim. Aggie knew she could go anywhere in this dress and no one would take her for a servant.

She couldn't speak.

"Oh, it's beautiful" she said at last. "I never owned anything so beautiful." She ran her hand over the soft fabric.

"Try it on for us, dearie. We'd like to see you in it," Mrs. MacDougall said. A few minutes later, returning from the pantry where she'd slipped the dress on, Aggie caught sight of herself in the hall mirror. Why, I'm almost pretty! she thought before she could tell herself not to be vain. But Mrs. MacDougall and Ritchie were extravagant in their praise.

"There," Ritchie exclaimed, "did I no tell you it would fit? She looks like a young princess."

"Aye, Ritchie, I didn'a believe anyone could be so slim, but she is. Agnes, my child, you look beautiful. You'll have no trouble finding a husband in Canada," she joked. Aggie blushed.

As Aggie left Mrs. MacDougall's house that evening, the two old ladies fought back their tears and made her promise to write. She half dreaded, half hoped that Davy would be under the lamp across the street as usual. But the darkening street was empty.

Feeling empty as the street, Aggie started home alone in a light rain, carrying the box with the dress under her arm. She tried to tell herself it wasn't fair to expect Davy, that she had no right to feel so disappointed. But that didn't change the way she felt. She was more than halfway home when she heard footsteps ringing in the street behind her. It was Davy, breathless from running.

"I couldn'a let you leave without saying goodbye, Aggie," he managed to gasp. One look at his cheerful, handsome face was all Aggie needed. The parcel fell to the ground, and she threw herself onto the damp roughness of Davy's jacket.

"Oh Davy, I'm sorry, I'm sorry," she said and she began to cry. But if anyone had asked her what she was sorry for she couldn't have said.

Davy stroked her hair and let her cry.

"Whist you, Aggie," he said finally. "It's no the end of the world," and he gave her his handkerchief. "I've something for you to remember me by," he said, "and because it's your birthday tomorrow." Reaching into his coat pocket he brought out a small velvet box.

The brooch inside was fashioned into the graceful shape of a silver swallow, set with dozens of tiny, silvery-black stones. It flashed, even in this fading light. Aggie knew the stones were marcasite. Rich women didn't wear marcasite, they wore jewels. Even so, the pin was more than Davy could afford. It was the first piece of jewellery Aggie had ever owned. She looked at him with new tears in her eyes.

"No tears now, Aggie. Let me remember you as my strong and cheerful lass."

"Thank you, Davy, it's beautiful."

"It reminded me of you," he said, and he kissed her on the forehead. It was the only time he ever kissed her.

From then on, it was so difficult to accept what was happening that Aggie felt she was watching herself from a great distance. The figure that went through the motions of eating that last meal with her family, of lying in her bed awake for most of the night, of rising early to say goodbye to her mother in the dark before dawn, might have been a puppet or an actress in the picture shows. Her heart seemed to have turned into something that was cold and heavy, and could not really feel.

In the morning, Aggie was glad to leave before first light. At least she wouldn't have to face the young ones again. Jen had clung to her the night before and cried herself to sleep. Now Aggie choked down the breakfast her mother insisted she eat. Then it was time to go. Just before Aggie left, her mother handed her a small brown envelope.

"We wanted you to have this, Aggie. There's one for Emma too." Inside were two postcard-sized photographs of her younger brothers and sisters. They stared straight at the camera, solemn and still, looking nothing like themselves.

Aggie couldn't imagine where her mother had found the money.

"Thank you, Mum," she said, slipping the photos back into their envelope. "I'll take good care of them." As they hugged goodbye, Aggie realized how thin her mother was beneath her faded cotton dress.

Then it was just Aggie and her father. One of his friends had borrowed a car to take them to the docks in Glasgow, an hour's drive. Aggie still could not forgive her father for beating the little ones. She climbed into the back seat without speaking, leaving him to sit in front with his chum.

"Well, Agnes, off on your big adventure?" her father's friend asked with a grin as soon as they were on the road.

"Aye, Mr. Munro," Aggie said. And that was all. She did not want to be drawn into a conversation that would include her father. From the front seat, her father turned and gave her a sharp look. Aggie looked away. The two men fell easily into a conversation about the mines.

Leaving Loughlinter on this road, they passed the cemetery where Dougie was buried. Aggie suddenly realized she'd almost forgotten her brother in the past few days. Now she was leaving and she hadn't even visited his grave. The black iron fence of cemetery was passing quickly. Could she ask the men to stop? No, there wasn't time. In any case, she was afraid her father would think she was daft, wasting Mr. Munro's time. Then the cemetery was gone. Goodbye, Dougie, she thought, goodbye. She was glad the men were absorbed in their conversation. Neither of them noticed when she slipped her handkerchief out of her purse and quickly wiped her eyes.

Aggie had never been on such a long ride before, but the fields and villages were mostly hidden in a grey winter drizzle. When they finally reached Glasgow, tall buildings crowded along both sides of the streets. The ship, when they came to the quay, was large and black, alive with sailors and passengers, bright with lights in the mist. There was hardly any time left.

Douglas Maxwell was not a man who put great store in words, but now he spoke.

"Aggie, I know how hard this is for you, lass. I want you to know that your mother and I..." he began, but Aggie would not raise her eyes and his voice trailed off. Still, Aggie did not look up. "Well, we thank you, lass, for doing this," Douglas Maxwell said quickly. "I dinna blame you for being angry. God go with you." He turned and was gone.

She wanted to cry out then, "Wait, Da!" She wanted to tell him that she wasn't angry about going to Canada, that she was glad to be able to help. But he had already disappeared into the noise and confusion and piles of cargo. He had to get back, Aggie knew. Time was money. She mounted the gang-plank alone and found her cabin, deep in the hold of the ship. Then she stood on the deck and watched as the ship lurched out of its moorings.

Somewhere on deck, a young woman began to sing. Her voice carried, high and thin over the cool morning air as she sang,

> So fair thee well, my own true love,
> So deep in love am I,
> That I will come again, my dear
> Though t'were ten thousand miles.

Aggie knew the song. It was "My Love is Like a Red, Red Rose" by Robbie Burns, the great poet. And she knew the singer was promising to return. Would Aggie ever return? No, she couldn't imagine she would. My heart stays here, Aggie thought. I'm being torn in two. Glasgow disappeared from sight as the boat sailed down the River Clyde to the sea.

Aggie had hoped that travelling by ship would be something like the seaside holidays other girls sometimes took — no work and fresh, salt air. She wasn't prepared for the oily smell and constant noise of the ship's engine. Was it that or the roll of the sea that made her so ill? Maybe neither. But seasickness gave her a good excuse to lie on her bunk and cry, and that was all she wanted to do.

The three other girls who shared the cramped cabin were strangers, on their way to Canada to work as domestics too. One had come aboard when the ship stopped in Londonderry, Ireland, one day out of Glasgow. Determined to make the most of this short holiday, they had little time for Agnes. Even the matron, whose job it was to care for young girls travelling to Canada alone, simply looked in on Aggie once and said, "You'll live." Aggie gave up on eating and survived on water. She was wretchedly miserable, the seasickness and homesickness blended together so that she could not tell where one ended and the other began.

Then, late one afternoon, Inid, the Irish girl, said, "You can see land now. Not Canada, but Newfoundland. We'll be in Halifax in another day or two." Aggie pulled herself out of her bunk, longing to see land. She made her way to the deck on rubbery legs. Not too far away she could see high, rocky cliffs. Could anyone live there? she wondered. Then, as night fell, she saw lights that must come from little villages, strung along the coastline like a few bright beads on a necklace.

Somehow that helped. She went back to her bunk and slept soundly. Towards morning, she dreamed that she and Dougie were standing on the deck of the ship as it sailed into a harbour. In the dream, Aggie felt they were coming home. The next day, the sea grew calmer. Aggie felt better and was finally able to eat. But the other girls had formed their groups. It was too late to make friends.

They sailed into Halifax the next day in a cold, grey dawn. The size of the harbour amazed Aggie and the houses stacked up on the hills all looked new. The sun came up, the morning fog lifted, and the fresh snow turned an unbelievable, fairy tale pink against the bright, blue water. The world was not old and grey as it had been in Scotland, but fresh and new. For the first time since she'd left her mother, Aggie felt her heart lift.

Then everyone was herded off the boat and made to wait in long lines to clear immigration, like cattle at a marketplace. Aggie still felt the roll of the sea under her feet. She had to lean against something; otherwise she was afraid she'd lose her footing. In line ahead of her, a young woman was struggling to keep her small daughter and baby quiet. Thinking of her brothers and sisters, Aggie reached down and lifted the little girl onto the wooden railing.

"Hullo," she said. "I'm Aggie. Who are you."

"I'm Elsie," said the child, "and this is Maggie." She held up an old knitted doll. She pointed to the baby, "That's our Robert, and my Mum. We're going to Canada to our Da."

The tired-looking young woman smiled at Aggie.

"I told her this is Canada, but she wouldn'a believe me because her father isn'a here. He's in Montreal."

"He said he'd meet us in Canada," the child said solemnly. She was, Aggie guessed, about four. Small for her age and serious like Jen.

"Well, Elsie, I'm sure he will. Would you like a sweet?" Aggie found a mint in her purse, the last of Jen's ill-gotten candy, given to Aggie as a going away present when no one was looking. Elsie opened her mouth like a baby bird and Aggie popped it in.

"My, this line is long and slow," the child's mother said. "I imagine we'll be here all day. I'm Marion...Marion Ballantyne." She was small and pretty and her blond hair was bobbed fashionably short.

"Agnes Maxwell," Aggie said. Suddenly she realized how little she knew about meeting people. Surely she ought to say something more, but what?

"Are you coming to Canada to meet your Da too?" Elsie asked.

Aggie laughed.

"No, Elsie, my Da is at home in Scotland. I'm coming to Canada to see my sister Emma, and to work as a servant in someone's home."

"Oh, Mum," Elsie said, "could she no come and work in our home? I'd like that."

Marion smiled.

"It will be some time, Elsie Ballantyne, before we can afford help at home, my pet."

"In any case, Elsie, my sister is in Toronto," Aggie added, "I'm travelling on to there."

"Oh," Elsie said. She looked downcast.

"Do you know much about Toronto?" Marion asked. Aggie shook her head.

"I've no idea what Montreal will be like," Marion said. "Angus works as a clerk in the railway headquarters there. He left Scotland six months ago, just after Robbie was born, to come ahead and find us a place to live. He wrote me twice a week, but you know how men are. He's never said a word about the city or even what sort of place we'll be living in. Of course, we're so glad to be going to him we'd live in a tent if we had to, wouldn't we Elsie?"

The child nodded, then after a moment said, "A tent made of canvas, Mum, or one of buffalo skins?"

Aggie and Marion laughed.

Just then, a woman in a Red Cross uniform came over.

"I'll take you and the children to the nursery, ma'am," she said. "You can rest there 'til it's your turn."

Aggie was sad to see them leave. Suddenly she heard Marion say, "Could I no bring my sister? She's a great help with the wee ones." To Aggie's shock the Red Cross woman looked back at her.

"Well, normally we say only mothers and children. But if she's your sister, I guess so," she said.

"Come along then, sis," Marion said, winking when the woman's back was turned. Aggie was so astonished she could only follow.

The nursery was just as dingy as the big waiting room. There were hardly any windows, and the wooden walls were stained a dark colour that seemed to drain the light from the room. A sign high up on the wall said:

**Red Cross Juniors
WELCOME YOU
To Canada.**

The room was bare except for a row of white metal cribs, a few low tables and some chairs, but at least they could sit down. After Marion nursed her baby, a woman brought some tea. Aggie helped Elsie find a few battered toys, including a chipped china doll's cup. Elsie was delighted. "Now Maggie can have a drop of tea as well," she cried. "Maggie loves her tea."

Finally, they were called to go through immigration. After all that waiting, Aggie was surprised to find she had only to show her immigration papers, passport, and vaccination certificate.

"That's that," said the immigration officer, stamping her papers and handing them back. "Wait over there please." He indicated a crowd of other girls. Aggie recognized some of them from the boat.

"What happens next, please?" she asked.

"You're off to the station, missy," the man replied. "Your luggage is already there. Train leaves in about an hour."

Aggie had expected time to rest. Time to adjust to dry land. This was a surprise. The old bus that took them to the train station was so dirty with mud and slush that Aggie could hardly see out the windows, so she saw nothing of Halifax close up.

Not long after, everyone was ushered into the train. These cars were used for immigrants alone, it seemed. The seats were bare boards. Aggie stood in the doorway while others pushed by her. The car was heated, poorly, by a small, pot-bellied stove. The air smelled of wet wool and disappointment. Suddenly, in her mind, Aggie saw a clean bed that did not move — a bed with little Jen curled up warmly in it. The memory seemed ancient and dim. Her eyes began to sting with tears. She felt a tap on her shoulder. It was Marion.

"Come with me, Agnes. We've got four seats together." Aggie followed her thankfully.

The four seats were in a corner of the car, one of the best spots on the train.

"The conductor saved them for me," Marion explained. "This is the railway Angus works for. He wanted us to wait in Halifax a few days. He could get us better tickets then, on a fancy train. What did we write to him, Elsie?" Marion said, turning to the child who had already snuggled beside Aggie.

"That we'd rather walk to Montreal," the child said stoutly.

Marion laughed.

"Indeed we did. We told him we'd walk if that would get us to him sooner. And so we would. No fancy trains are going to keep us from him a day longer than we've already waited."

"Indeed they will not," said the child at Aggie's side.

As train pulled out of the station, Elsie laid her head on Aggie's lap. Soon she was asleep. The constant rumble of the train, the gentle rocking motion, the warm child's steady breathing were irresistible. Aggie closed her eyes and slept too.

When Aggie woke, it was already dark outside. The train chugged on into the night, the whistle blowing long and mournfully at every level crossing. The conductor brought food to Marion and her children, and no money changed hands. Marion shared her food with Aggie. Later, everyone settled down to sleep wherever they could. Some of the more adventurous ones even climbed into the overhead luggage racks. Blankets came for Marion and her children, and even a few pillows. Marion did not pretend that Aggie was her sister again, but shared what she was given.

When Aggie opened her eyes in the morning, the train was carrying them through forests of bare, black trees swathed in deep snow. Aggie never imagined that any place could be as big and empty as Canada seemed. Later they passed snowy farmers' fields that looked like blank, white pages.

Marion talked about everything. When Elsie and Robert were napping, she told Aggie how she met her husband.

"I was working in a shop, a milliner's, supposed to be learning how to make hats, but I was all thumbs. Angus came in to buy his mother a hat for her birthday." She showed Aggie a photo of a small, dapper-looking man with a neat mustache and smiling eyes, then carefully returned it to her purse. "A week later, he was back again. A hat for his sister this time. Well, when he came back the third time, I began to wonder if it was really the hats he was after. Angus is not a bold man. He bought four hats before he was brave enough to ask me out. After we were married, I found the last one tucked away in a closet." Marion smiled, then frowned.

"My father didn'a want me to marry. Not just Angus, but anyone. My mother died, you see, when I was just twelve. But I told him, you'll no stop me. Angus is the man I mean to marry. So of course he had to change his mind."

Aggie imagined her father forbidding her to marry someone he disapproved of. Would she be able to do what Marion had done? She didn't think so.

"Angus is such a good father," Marion continued, "such a good husband. I've missed him these months. I'm tired of sleeping alone." Then, noticing Aggie's discomfort she added, "You know, Aggie, it's lovely to lie with the man you love." Aggie had never heard anyone talk that way. She blushed to the roots of her hair. Marion only laughed. "Someday you'll believe me," she said. Then Elsie woke up.

While Aggie listened to Marion and played with Elsie, the land outside the train went on and on. By late afternoon, the tracks ran along the ice-clogged St. Lawrence River. It was bigger and more grand than any river Aggie had ever seen. They passed small towns and villages now. Aggie was relieved to see that Canada was not quite so empty as it had seemed. Then they stopped across the river from a city built on high cliffs.

"Oh, Mum," Elsie cried, "look...look at the castle! Does a queen live there? Can we visit the queen?"

Aggie looked across the river. There did seem to be a castle. When they asked the conductor, he laughed and said it was a hotel called the Chateau Frontenac, and the city was Quebec City. Late that evening they came to Montreal.

"There's my Da," Elsie cried as the train slowed by the platform.

"Well," said the conductor who was helping them gather their bags, "your father must be pretty special. It isn't just anyone who gets to meet the trains."

"My Da is the specialest," Elsie cried, and she was off with the conductor, forgetting to say goodbye to Aggie in her excitement.

Marion turned to Aggie and kissed her cheek as best she could with the sleeping baby in her arms.

"Safe journey, Agnes," she said and she was gone. Suddenly, the train seemed just as dismal as it had when Aggie first boarded in Halifax.

The conductor returned alone.

"Everyone travelling on collect your luggage please," he said. "We'll change trains in a few minutes."

Aggie got her suitcase, then gathered one of the blankets from the seat and hugged it to her. It smelled the way a baby smells, of milk and sweet, new skin. She held the blanket until it was time to change trains.

The new train was just the same — drafty with hard wooden seats. Some time in the night, while Aggie slept fitfully, the train left Quebec and entered Ontario. The next morning when she opened her eyes, Aggie saw what seemed to be a great, grey ocean through the window.

"Is that the sea?" she asked the conductor, and he laughed.

"Not the sea, only Lake Ontario."

"Is Toronto near then?"

"We'll be there in no time."

From the train, Toronto looked poor at first, full of badly made houses on narrow streets. Aggie was beginning to worry when she saw wider streets and a few tall, grey buildings. Finally, the train stopped. The conductor called, "Toronto!" But they seemed to be in the middle of a vast field of tracks, with no station in sight. There must be some mistake, Aggie thought, and she stayed in her seat.

"Toronto, miss," the conductor said. "You get off here."

"But where's the station?" Aggie asked.

The man chuckled.

"It's over there. I'm afraid it's a bit of a hike. We'll bring your baggage along presently. They finished the new station last year, but they're having a bit of trouble deciding who should build a viaduct to get the passengers into it. In the meantime, everyone walks over the tracks. I'm sorry," he said, and he helped her leave the train.

Aggie made her way across the tracks, dozens of them it seemed, following the crowd. Finally they reached the station. Union Station was the biggest building Aggie had ever seen. Footsteps echoed from the marble floors to high, vaulted ceilings. The place was bathed in the weak winter sunlight that streamed in through high windows. It looked like a cathedral. These people, she thought, must worship trains. But her thought was cut short when someone grabbed her arm. There stood Emma in a new-looking tweed coat and fur-lined boots.

Aggie and Emma had never been as close as sisters might be. But here, alone in this new country, Aggie secretly hoped all that might change, that she and Emma would be friends.

"Well, Aggie, you made the trip alone and you look to be in one piece. You've more courage than I gave you credit for." This was not praise, but a kind of challenge. That was Emma. But at least she knew what to do. Taking her younger sister in tow, Emma spoke to the harried lady from the Travellers' Aid Society who was rounding up all the young domestics she could find. She was more than happy to entrust Aggie to this smart young girl who knew her way.

And then they were out on the street. Just opposite Union Station, steel girders towered, the framework of a great, new building. High in the air, men walked cross the beams as if they were walking down city streets. It made Aggie dizzy just to watch.

"What's that?" she asked.

"Fancy new hotel," Emma replied. "They're calling it the Royal York."

The frosty air bit Aggie's nose and her toes soon went numb inside her thin leather shoes. The banks of ice that lined the sidewalks were old and flecked with soot. As they waited for the tram, Emma handed her a ticket.

"For the streetcar," she explained. Streetcar? Aggie wondered if Emma was teasing.

The streetcar rumbled up. It was smaller than the trams at home. In spite of the winter coating of slush, Aggie saw it was also newer. Like the lovely cathedral station, everything looked new, as if Toronto had been invented the day before Aggie's arrival. The streetcar was warmer than the train from Halifax. Not until they settled themselves in seats did Aggie think to ask where they were going.

"To the hostel they run for girls like us at College Street. Just until you find a position, and they'll help you with that. It's all set up, you see, to make sure we find our way into the kitchens of the well-to-do, and not out on the streets."

Aggie recognized her father's bitterness in Emma's voice. Neither could accept authority or control without resentment, though Emma knew how to hide this when she had to. But to Aggie this system sounded just fine. How else would girls like her ever find their way in this vast city?

The streetcar turned and Emma told her they were now on Yonge Street, one of the main streets of Toronto. Shoe shops, glove shops, china shops, and furriers lined the street. They looked so fine, with fresh paint on the woodwork and gold-edged lettering in the windows. Then the streetcar passed two enormous shops that stood opposite each other, with huge, plate glass windows and brass revolving doors.

"Eaton's and Simpson's," Emma told her. "The two biggest shops in the city. I'll take you some day on our half day if you like," she said. "Remember to take your half day on Thursday, like me. Otherwise, you'll roam around like some lost lamb."

Just before they reached College Street, Aggie remembered Flora's story. She noticed vapour coming up through the grates in the streets. Although the snow was piled in banks on the sidewalks, the streets themselves were dry and clear.

"Emma," she said, "do they heat the streets?"

Emma gave her a look of pure scorn.

"Heat the streets? Are you daft?"

"But steam comes out of the grates..." Aggie faltered.

"Och, that's just vapour from the storm sewers. Heat the streets indeed!"

Times change. Places change. But sisters, Aggie reflected, do not.

Chapter Four

The Stockwoods

The milk wagon passed every morning before six. Now that the snow had melted, the clip-clop of horses' hooves always woke Aggie. She was glad, because that gave her time to collect herself before the alarm clock went off. At least there was some light in the sky now. It would certainly be spring in Loughlinter, but here in Canada winter was slow in passing — it was March now and still no sign of warm weather. This room in the Stockwood house had been Aggie's home for two weeks, an attic room with sloping ceilings and a little diamond-shaped window. Through the window, Aggie could see nearby branches of the great maples that soared far above the roof. The buds were fat and red with life. Maybe spring was on the way.

Emma had offered to find her a position in Rosedale near her own, but, after travelling from Scotland alone, Aggie found she was less willing to be led and dominated by her sister. So Employment Services had sent her here to the Stockwood house for an interview.

Aggie remembered walking in from the streetcar stop that first day. Her thin leather shoes did nothing to protect her feet from the new snow that had fallen. But she almost

forgot the cold, looking at the beautiful houses in this neighbourhood called Deer Park. Some of these homes were larger
than the finest house in Loughlinter. Finally, she found the
address that matched the one Employment Services had
given her. The house was large and made of sombre brown
brick. The roof was steep and the windows were filled with
little diamonds of latticed glass that managed to wink even
on this overcast morning. On one side of the house was a
glass sunroom. Aggie had walked up the snowy driveway to
the back entrance, her feet almost beyond pain. The woman
who had answered the door was red-faced, tall, and unsmil-
ing. She gave Aggie a cold, appraising look before opening
the door wide enough to let her in.

"I'm Mrs. Bradley," she said shortly. "Mrs. Stockwood is
in the dining room. Wipe your feet well on that mat and wait
while I tell her you're here."

Aggie was left alone in the big, bright kitchen. She stood
because Mrs. Bradley had not invited her to sit. In this
warmth, her feet thawed and promptly began to throb as if
they were on fire. She looked around to take her mind off the
pain. The walls were lined with mint-green cupboards that
reached right up to the high ceilings. Beside a spotless, white
enamel sink stood something Aggie had only ever seen in
magazines: an electric stove. A loud whirring noise startled
her, and she realized that the black and white enamelled
cabinet near her must be a refrigerator. Mrs. MacDougall still
had an icebox. Aggie's family had neither.

After what seemed like an eternity, Mrs. Bradley returned.

"Follow me," she said.

A swinging door led to the dining room where a small
woman in a blue and green print dress sat reading the
morning paper and drinking tea from a china cup. Her grey

hair was bobbed and waved. Unlike Mrs. Bradley she did smile.

"So, you're Agnes Maxwell. I'm Mrs. Stockwood. You're just over from Scotland, Miss Dunlop at Employment Services told me. Is that right?"

"Aye, ma'am, that's correct," Aggie said.

Mrs. Stockwood's smile grew wider. She turned to her housekeeper who stood just behind her.

"Oh, isn't that just the most charming accent, Mrs. Bradley?" she asked. Mrs. Bradley tried, but apparently could not coax her face into any semblance of agreement.

"You have your reference?" Mrs. Stockwood asked.

Aggie dug into her purse for Mrs. MacDougall's letter. The sight of the familiar, spidery handwriting brought a lump to her throat. As Mrs. Stockwood read, Aggie looked around the dining room. A bank of windows filled with those leaded diamonds of glass occupied most of one wall. On a bright day, Aggie guessed, the morning sun would fill this room. Opposite the windows was a white marble fireplace, even now laid with fresh wood and kindling, not an ash in sight. Mrs. Stockwood looked rather lost, sitting alone at the vast dining room table. Now she looked up.

"My, this is excellent. It's a wonder your former employer let you leave. We have been so anxious to obtain the services of a British maid," Mrs. Stockwood told Aggie. "Anyone who really cares about quality of service has one now. I'm quite the last among my friends. Can you start today?"

"Miss Dunlop said you could telephone to have my things sent from the hostel," Aggie told her. "I can start now if you like."

"Wonderful. I notice from your reference that you didn't live in."

"No, ma'am. I always lived at home." Somehow that last word did not catch in her throat.

"Well, I'm sure you'll be happy here. You'll have your half days, Thursdays and Sundays. Your salary is twenty-five dollars a month. Now we'll have to order uniforms. Tell Mrs. Bradley your size and she'll see to that. Mrs. Bradley, show...Agnes, is it?...show Agnes her room, give her a cup of tea and put her to work."

"Thank you," Aggie had said, but when she tried to move, her feet wouldn't work. What began as a step ended in a limp.

"Goodness," Mrs. Stockwood said, "have you hurt yourself?"

"It's just the cold, Mrs. Stockwood," Aggie said. "It hurts my feet."

Mrs. Stockwood looked at Aggie's feet.

"You mean to say no one has provided you with boots?"

Aggie shook her head. She had no money for boots. None of the secondhand boots at the hostel had fit her. Emma had promised to look for boots, but Aggie hadn't seen her since.

"You poor child. It's a wonder you didn't get frostbite. Mrs. Bradley, aren't my old boots from last year still in the closet? Remember? You thought you might send them home to your sister's family."

Mrs. Bradley nodded.

"I meant to, as soon as I could get to the post office," she said. Mrs. Stockwood didn't seem to notice that her housekeeper's voice tightened around those words.

"Well, this will save you the trip. Agnes's feet look small. I'm sure those boots will do for her." To Aggie's surprise, Mrs. Stockwood rose. "Let's look. Agnes, for heaven's sake, sit down."

Astonished, Aggie had sat on the edge of a dining room chair while Mrs. Stockwood and Mrs. Bradley disappeared. A few minutes later, they returned, Mrs. Stockwood holding the boots triumphantly.

"Here they are. Try them on."

Mrs. Bradley had the look of a dog who just lost a bone.

The boots were heavy black felt with sturdy rubber soles. They fit perfectly.

"There," Mrs. Stockwood said. "Your feet are the same size as mine. Keep them. Now you may go and settle in."

Aggie had followed the silent Mrs. Bradley up to the attic. The pain in her feet was beginning to subside. The housekeeper showed Aggie the little attic room and handed her an armload of bedding she had picked up on the way.

"Make your bed and come back to the kitchen. There's plenty to do."

She did not mention the boots, but something of her stayed behind after she left, dark and disapproving as a shadow. A small voice inside Aggie told her she should leave now and go back to Employment Services. But she looked down at her shoes, salt stained, cracked, and soaked with melted snow, then at the boots she still held in her hand. Whatever this feeling was, it wasn't enough to send her out into the snow in those shoes again.

Even the attic in this house was warm. The mattress looked old and lumpy, but the bed stood alone in a quiet room. Aggie had not slept in a room without strangers since she left home almost two weeks before. She had never had a room of her own.

She'd put the boots on the floor, put the bedding on the bed and took the photo of her brothers and sisters out of her purse, propping it against the alarm clock that sat on a wobbly bedside table. Twenty-five dollars is what Emma makes, she thought. The sooner I get to work, the sooner I can send money home. Five dollars may be enough for me. The other twenty I'll send home.

When Aggie had returned to the kitchen, nothing more was said about a cup of tea.

"It's been weeks since we've had extra help in this house," Mrs. Bradley said. "There's plenty to do. I'll show you the broom closet." And she had. "Dust mop the upstairs, then I'll show you the laundry room. There's plenty of ironing." She gave Aggie one last look. "I hope you're honest," she'd said shortly. "The last girl we had was a liar and a thief."

Aggie had set to work at once, working as hard as she could. But Mrs. Bradley remained tight-lipped and unapproving.

On her first morning in the Stockwood house, when Aggie came down for breakfast, she'd found a slice of unbuttered toast waiting for her. The smell of bacon had made her mouth water. A slice of toast was not enough for breakfast. Aggie didn't feel she could ask Mrs. Bradley for butter and she wasn't bold enough to get it herself. Perhaps, she thought, when Mrs. Bradley leaves the kitchen to serve breakfast, I can dip my toast into the bacon fat on the stove. But Aggie had known that wouldn't really help. She wouldn't stay if she couldn't eat properly, boots or no boots. She was just trying to decide how to get back to Employment Services when Mrs. Stockwood had entered the kitchen.

"Mrs. Bradley," she said, "I almost forgot about my bridge club this week. Be sure to order extra bread and eggs when you put in the grocery order, and a tin of those shrimp please."

Then she had glanced at Aggie.

"Surely that's not your breakfast. Don't you feel well?" she asked.

Aggie didn't know what to say. Before she could stop herself, her eyes travelled to Mrs. Bradley's back. Mrs. Stockwood followed her gaze, and Aggie saw she understood. Aggie held her breath.

"Mrs. Bradley, I know how busy you are in the mornings. I'm sure Agnes is able to scramble an egg for herself...aren't you, dear?" Aggie nodded. "Good. I seem to remember a little frying pan Rodney sometimes uses when he cooks for himself." She opened the cupboard. "Yes, here it is. And the eggs are in the refrigerator. Have one every morning, if you like. Have two." She was about to leave the kitchen, but turned back. "Oh, Mrs. Bradley, did you order those uniforms?"

"Yes, Mrs. Stockwood, they'll be delivered this afternoon."

"Excellent. I'd like Agnes to serve at my bridge club on Friday." After she left the room, Mrs. Bradley had slammed the frying pan down so hard it made Aggie jump. But nothing was said.

Now, in the chill of the morning, Aggie slipped quickly into one of the uniforms that had arrived that day, a plain black dress. Pulling her thick, fair hair into a knot at the back of her neck, she added a little white headband, worn fashionably low on her forehead. The white aprons that completed her uniform were kept in the kitchen. She glanced quickly around the room to see that everything was tidy. Every morning for the past two weeks Aggie told herself: today I will find a way to prove to Mrs. Bradley I belong here. So far, she knew, she hadn't.

Mrs. Bradley was already frying bacon when Aggie entered the kitchen. Avoiding her, Aggie took a small bowl from the cupboard and broke an egg into it. As Mrs. Bradley moved away from the stove, Aggie set to work making her own breakfast — the scrambled eggs she had eaten every morning since that first. Chicken eggs — not the little pigeon eggs Aggie had rarely eaten in Scotland. These breakfasts helped because Aggie's portions at lunch and supper were often far too small. Mrs. Bradley still seemed angry with Aggie. It had to be more than the boots or a few eggs.

The Stockwoods seemed nice though. Mr. Stockwood was a banker who worked in an office on King Street. He was as kindly and cheerful as his wife and even asked Aggie about her family in Scotland. But the Stockwoods were busy people. Aggie knew they seldom gave her a second thought. Her only real friend in the house was the old cat, Duchess. Aggie had never liked cats, but this one was black, tan, and orange with fur as soft as a rabbit's, deep green eyes, and gentle ways. She would sit and purr and listen to Aggie's homesick stories of her family and Loughlinter and sometimes try to sit on the paper when Aggie wrote her letters home. In these letters, Aggie pretended she was happy. Her mother had enough to worry about.

At least today was Thursday. Aggie could forget all this and spend the afternoon with Emma and her friends. Mrs. Bradley left the kitchen with the Stockwoods' breakfast and Aggie sat down to eat. When Mrs. Bradley returned, Aggie was already washing the dishes.

"When you finish those, you can start on young Rodney's room," Mrs. Bradley said, stacking dishes beside the sink without looking at her. "Exams at Queen's will be over in a few weeks, and we're expecting him home. The missus wants his room out of the way before we start the regular spring cleaning. Rodney gets wheezy if there's dust. Take down the drapes, then dust and pack all the books. There's cartons in the basement. The painters will be in on Monday."

Aggie knew Rodney Stockwood only from the pictures she dusted, one in the main hall and one on the sitting room mantel. Aggie guessed he was a few years older than she was, a thin-faced and serious looking young man with wire-rimmed glasses and hair that was already thinning on top. She knew he was the Stockwoods' second child and only son. An older daughter lived far to the west in Regina with a husband and two small children of her own. Mrs. Stock-wood, and even Mrs. Bradley, always talked of Rodney as if he were made of glass and nothing was too good for him. He was studying at Queen's University, in a place called Kingston. Aggie had actually passed through there on the train from Halifax, but late at night so she had no impression of the place. From his photos and what she heard, Aggie imagined Rodney would be a dull and somewhat spoiled young man who would expect to have everything just so.

Rodney's room was, like almost every room in the house, bright and spacious. Aggie worked there all morning. By standing on the cast iron radiator, she managed to get the heavy drapes down alone. Bookshelves lined one whole wall. She dusted the books and packed them into boxes in preparation for the painters, wondering how anyone could possibly read so much. By noon, most of the heavy boxes were stacked in a spare room. After lunch she changed into a dress of her own and left the house without saying goodbye to anyone, happy to leave Mrs. Bradley behind.

Well, almost happy. As she approached the corner of Yonge and Bloor where Emma had arranged to meet, Aggie realized, not for the first time, that she didn't quite know what to make of Emma's friends. Like Emma, they all worked in houses in Rosedale. The Stockwoods were wealthy by Aggie's standards, but the families in Rosedale sounded richer still. Some employed three or even four servants. From talking to Emma's friends, Aggie realized their lives were much livelier. They even visited back and forth among the houses after work in the evenings. As far as Aggie knew, this was unheard of in Deer Park. Or maybe it was just that Mrs. Bradley would never allow it.

Emma seemed to show up with different girls every week. Aggie had trouble keeping track of them. Millie or Molly, Polly or Penny, Aggie was never really sure who she was talking to. This brief release from the "yes ma'ams" and "no ma'ams" of their working lives made them giddy and reckless for these few hours. To Aggie, they resembled nothing so much as a flock of birds — all chatter and flap.

One recognized Aggie as she approached.

"Eeh, Emma," she cried, "'ere comes your sis. Now we can get going." This girl was Millie (or was it Molly?). In any case, her broad accent told Aggie that she was from Liverpool.

Emma greeted Aggie with a smile.

"But we still haven't decided where to go," said one small girl Aggie thought might be called Sally.

"I want to go see that new Greta Garbo picture," Emma said decidedly. "Look," she pointed to the newspaper in her hand, *"The Divine Woman."*

"Greta Garbo, isn't she swell?" said another girl Aggie didn't recognize at all.

Sally looked over Em's shoulder.

"That's all the way down on King Street," she said.

"We can take the streetcar."

Sally looked stricken.

"If I spend another seven cents, I won't have enough to get in to the show." Everyone looked dejected. No one could spare the extra seven cents for Sally's fare and no one had an extra ticket either.

Emma glanced at the paper again.

"We can walk," she said. "There's time."

No one tried to argue. It had always been that way. Leave Emma with other girls and in a few hours every one would be doing just what she wanted. The day was grey but not too cold. Aggie was fascinated by Yonge Street. She enjoyed looking in the windows they passed — florists, caterers, shoe shops, everything looked so lovely. Emma took her arm, friendly now that she had her way.

"Tell me what you've been doing," she said. The other girls seemed content to listen.

Aggie wanted to tell Em about Mrs. Bradley. But this was not the time, so she began to talk about the preparations for Rodney Stockwood's return.

"A university student," Molly said. "You'll have to mind yourself with 'im around." The other girls giggled.

Aggie was mystified.

"Why?"

"Oh, you know. Them young men only 'as one thing on their minds," Molly said.

"Molly," Emma said sharply, "dinna frighten her."

"Forewarned is forearmed, my old mum always said," Molly continued, ignoring Emma. "A girl's got to know. You never can tell what might 'appen. Why there was a girl shot 'er employer dead right 'ere in Toronto, only about ten years ago."

Molly had everyone's attention now.

"What happened to her?" Sally asked.

"Nothing. Let 'er go they did, once she told them 'er story. Seems 'er missus took a trip and the mister started throwing wild parties, trying to have 'is way with 'er. Tried to bribe 'er with 'is own wife's silk stockings. The girl took 'is gun and shot 'im dead on 'is own doorstep. Nobody blamed 'er. And that's true."

Everyone was silent for a minute.

"Well," Emma said finally, "I'm sure that doesn'a happen every day."

"More often that we know, I'll warrant," Molly replied. "All these girls who end up walking the streets..."

"Molly!" Emma said.

"This isn't just some fancy of mine, Emma," Molly insisted. "Your sister's always lived at 'ome. She's never had to look out for 'erself before. Well, now she 'as to, 'asn't she?" She turned to Aggie. "Read the papers if you don't believe me. Some of them girls started off as domestics, same as us. What's a girl going to do when 'er employer tries to force 'imself on 'er? How is she to get 'er reference for another job? All downhill from there, I tell you. Is there a bolt on your door?" she asked.

"No," Aggie said, "just a plain door knob." She was feeling a bit weak and shaky.

"Well," Molly said, "I'd get one if I was you, dearie."

No one spoke, but Aggie saw that Emma was flushed with anger. Was this really something to worry about? She wouldn't be able to ask Emma until they were alone.

Now her sister turned to Sally.

"I can't wait for the talkies to come to Toronto," Emma said, pointedly changing the subject.

"Vitaphone," Sally said. "I read all about it in the papers. Do you think it will last? Pictures with sound? It seems like a good idea."

"Who can tell?" Emma replied. "Maybe it's just a fad. But I'd like to see one just the same."

"Just imagine hearing Valentino play his love scenes," Sally said and she put her hand up to her forehead in a mock swoon.

"Sally, Valentino died two years ago," someone said.

"Yes, but I mourn him still," Sally replied.

"You're fair daft, Sally," Emma said, but she smiled.

Aggie liked the picture shows. The cinemas in Toronto were done up like palaces with red carpets, chandeliers and gilt on the walls. It was nice to spend an afternoon sitting in a plush seat, watching someone else's problems.

It wasn't until much later that night, at bedtime, that Aggie thought back to what Molly had said. Did things like that really happen? Apparently so. She could hear Mr. and Mrs. Stockwood coming up the stairs for the night. Mr. Stockwood was always a gentleman. But what would Rodney be like? Aggie studied her door. Maybe she could prop a chair under the doorknob. At home, Aggie thought, I never worried about anything like this.

When the painters left and Rodney's room was back in order, spring cleaning began in earnest. Aggie's fancy black uniforms were put aside. She spent most days in a cotton wrapper with an old scarf tied over her hair while the big house was almost torn apart. Light fixtures were taken down and washed, walls washed or freshly papered. Plaster mouldings and the tops of doors were dusted — there was even a special brush for dusting radiators. The electric vacuum cleaner was not good enough for Mrs. Bradley now. Every rug that could be lifted was carried outside, put on the clothesline and beaten with a carpet-beater. On breezy days, the dust blew into Aggie's eyes. Two whole days were spent just cleaning the glass in the sunroom. Aggie washed all the wooden floors on her hands and knees, then polished them.

As the house looked brighter and cleaner Aggie felt more and more drained, as if the house were taking the energy from her. At night, when she lay in bed, she was so tired she felt as if a weight pressed her body into the mattress. She gave up going downtown on her half days. No one minded. They were all busy with spring cleaning too. Aggie spent Thursday afternoons in her room, curled up with one of Mrs. Stockwood's old magazines or writing letters home. Duchess would push her way past Aggie's half closed door and curl up, purring, at Aggie's feet, leaving only when she heard birds in the garden outside. Duchess loved to watch birds.

Sometimes, Aggie would catch the old cat up in her arms and cuddle into her soft fur. Once, she tried to pretend it was Jen she was holding. But it took more imagination than Aggie had to turn the old cat into her little sister.

Spring came. The maple trees opened, not with leaves as Aggie expected, but lacy green flowers. The windows of the house were flung wide to receive their sweet scent, and it seemed as if everyone and everything uncurled from a grey winter sleep. Even Aggie felt less tired. Spring cleaning was almost over.

The Stockwood house had a front staircase, broad and curved with a dark mahogany bannister. The stairs were deeply carpeted and the window was bright with three stained glass panels that showed a dark blue pond, green willows and a pale blue sky. A single blue-black swallow swooped through the centre panel. Mrs. Stockwood proudly showed these windows to visitors. Aggie understood why; they were beautiful. Sometimes, just for a moment, she would stop cleaning and look at the swallow, its dark wings arched gracefully in mid-flight. The swallow made her think of the marcasite brooch Davy had given her and of Davy himself. I would give anything, she thought, to see Davy slouched against a lamp post at the end of my day now.

The servants always used the narrow, dark stairs off the kitchen and Aggie was only allowed on the front staircase when cleaning, but it was her favourite place in the house. One bright April morning she stood there with the sun streaming in behind her, busy polishing the mahogany bannister with clean smelling wax. Suddenly the front door flew open and two suitcases skidded across the newly waxed floors. Behind them came a young man, tall and thin, wearing wire rimmed glasses. He could only be about twenty, but his blond hair was already thinning. He looked at Aggie, partly blinded by the light behind her, and blinked.

"A goddess in the guise of a maid!" he exclaimed. "However did you come to be here?"

Rodney Stockwood was home.

He left the hall without saying another word, and Aggie heard Mrs. Stockwood's delighted cry of surprise in the dining room. Remembering what Molly had said, Aggie wondered what Rodney meant, calling her a goddess. It sounded heathen.

Later, when Aggie went into the kitchen she was surprised to find Rodney sitting at the table with Mrs. Bradley.

"...and asparagus please," he was saying. "I haven't had asparagus since last spring. You wouldn't believe the food at Queen's, Mrs. B. Not fit to eat." Then he looked up. "Ah, the goddess of the staircase. Mrs. B, who is this lovely creature?"

To Aggie's amazement, Mrs. Bradley actually smiled.

"This is Agnes Maxwell," she said, "your mother's new maid."

Rodney rose and before Aggie could stop him, seized and actually kissed her hand.

"Any maid of mother's is a friend of mine."

Aggie blushed furiously. She had no idea what to say. Rodney noticed her discomfort.

"I haven't embarrassed you, have I? I certainly didn't mean to." Then he turned back to Mrs. Bradley. Aggie was immediately forgotten. She made a confused retreat.

What could she think of Rodney Stockwood? He was more cheerful and polite than Aggie had expected, and his presence certainly transformed Mrs. Bradley, but what did he mean by speaking so strangely and kissing her hand? She remembered Molly's prediction that university students could not be trusted. She wiped her hand where he had kissed it.

That afternoon in the hall she ran into Rodney again. He was coming out of his bedroom with a book in his hand. Aggie tried to slip past him, but he wouldn't let her.

"Mother tells me you did most of the work on my room. I really must thank you," he said. "It's never looked better." Again, Aggie didn't know what to say. Rodney went on. "You are a silent one, aren't you?"

That seemed to require a reply so Aggie said, "Aye, sir."

"Oh, please don't call me 'sir.' Call me 'Rodney'." He persisted in spite of Aggie's reticence: "Are you happy working here?"

This was unexpected. Again Aggie didn't know what to say. Anything she told him might be reported back to Mrs. Stockwood or even Mrs. Bradley.

"Please sir, Mr...Rodney," she said, "I dinna have time to stand here talking." She turned and left. But she thought about Rodney while she worked that afternoon. He seemed determined to bother her. Over the next few days, Rodney went out of his way to be friendly.

"Do you read, Agnes?" he asked her one morning when she was dusting the sitting room and came upon him bent over a book as usual.

"Only magazines, sir," she said. "Your mother gives me her *Chatelaine* sometimes when she's finished with it."

"Ah, I see. Not even romance novels? I have a friend who reads quite a lot of those," he said. "I could borrow some for you if you like."

Aggie shook her head.

"I'm too tired by the end of the day to read."

"I hadn't thought of that," Rodney said. For once, he seemed embarrassed.

Aggie didn't know what to make of Rodney, but she didn't bother to prop a chair under her door knob at night. He was a strange one, but he didn't seem the type to force himself on anyone.

Chapter Five

The Watch

When Aggie left the sitting room, she went to vacuum the master bedroom. Duchess regarded the vacuum cleaner as her personal enemy, spitting and hissing if it came anywhere near her. She had been sitting on Mr. Stockwood's dresser, watching the birds in the garden, but when she saw Aggie with the vacuum cleaner, she flew out of the room with a yowl.

That evening, as Aggie finished the dinner dishes, Mrs. Bradley came into the kitchen.

"You cleaned the master bedroom today, didn't you?"

"Aye," Aggie said, "I do it every other day."

"Did you notice anything valuable?" Mrs. Bradley asked.

Aggie thought for a moment. Mrs. Stockwood often left her rings on her bedside table. But not today.

"No," she replied, "nothing that I can remember."

"Nothing at all?" Mrs. Bradley looked at her with those hard grey eyes. Aggie shook her head.

"Mr. Stockwood forgot his wristwatch this morning. He thought he left it on his bedside table. It isn't there now. It isn't anywhere."

"I dusted that table," Aggie recalled. "There wasn'a any wristwatch."

"This is a valuable watch," Mrs. Bradley said. "It's identical to the one Rodney wears. Mrs. Stockwood bought them both last Christmas. You must know we would never tolerate a thief in this house. The girl who worked here before you was dismissed for stealing silverware."

Aggie felt herself redden.

"Mrs. Bradley, I've never stolen a penny in my life. What would I do with a man's watch?"

"There's plenty of pawnshops in this city," Mrs. Bradley said. "Now, Mrs. Stockwood is willing to make an exception this time. That's certainly more than I'd do. You put the watch back where you found it, and there'll be no questions asked. If not, you'll lose your place with us. There'll be no reference either."

"But I didn'a take the watch," Aggie said. "Why would I lie?"

"Well, I didn't take it and Rodney certainly didn't. We haven't had any workmen in the house since spring cleaning. That leaves you, doesn't it? You have until tomorrow. If it were up to me, I'd turn you out this minute."

Aggie was shaking when she left the kitchen, but her mind was clear. This was just about the worst thing that could possibly happen. If she were dismissed as a thief, no one else would hire her. She might even be shipped back to Scotland in disgrace. Carefully, in her mind, she went over every corner of the Stockwoods' bedroom. She was certain there had been no watch.

That night, Aggie dreamed she was in a huge jewellery shop, just like the Birks she and Emma had peered into one Thursday afternoon. But in the dream it was a pawnshop. A man came up to her and handed her Mr. Stockwood's watch.

When she looked up, it was Dougie. "Give it to him," he said. "Say you found it."

Aggie woke up feeling desolate and empty. It was Saturday. After breakfast Aggie was called into the dining room. Everyone was there; even Mrs. Bradley stood grimly by the table.

"Now, Agnes," Mrs. Stockwood began, "I'm sure this is just a little...mistake. Wouldn't you like to give us the watch, dear, so we can forget this ever happened?"

"But, Mrs. Stockwood," Aggie said, "I didn'a see a watch when I cleaned the bedroom yesterday. I thought about it last night. There wasn'a any watch. Plenty of times I've worked in that room with your rings lying about. If I were a thief, I'd have stolen one of them before now."

Rodney looked at Aggie. She met his gaze steadily for a long moment, then he spoke quietly.

"Mother, I believe her."

"Rodney, please don't interfere." Mr. Stockwood spoke for the first time.

There was an uncomfortable silence. Aggie could hardly believe this was happening.

"Anyone can see the girl is telling the truth," Rodney said after a moment. He threw his napkin on to the table and got up. "Let us repair to the scene of the alleged crime."

"Rodney, really, this is not a joking matter."

"I'm deadly serious, Father, I assure you. If the watch was not stolen, as Agnes maintains, it's still in the room."

Everyone followed Rodney to the bedroom.

"Father, where was the watch when you last saw it?"

"I believe it was on my bedside table," Mr. Stockwood said. Aggie could see he had little patience for this.

Rodney examined the bedside table with exaggerated care.

"Not here," he said at last. "Agnes, did you vacuum yesterday?"

"Aye, sir," Aggie said. Rodney looked at her with reproach when she said "sir."

"Could the watch have fallen onto the rug and been sucked up into the vacuum cleaner?" Rodney asked.

"It would have been mangled to pieces," Mrs. Bradley said.

"And it would have made a terrible noise," Aggie added.

"Did that happen?" asked Rodney hopefully. Aggie shook her head. Rodney seemed undaunted.

"Let us suppose, then, that the missing watch was not on the bedside table. Father, where else would you put your watch?"

"Really, Rodney, this is not a Sherlock Holmes mystery." Mr. Stockwood sighed and looked around. "On my dresser, I suppose."

"Ah, the dresser," Rodney said. He went over and looked under the dresser. "Nothing." Then he looked behind the dresser. "Very tight to the wall," he said. "Father, give me a hand." Mr. Stockwood helped him. When the dresser was pushed away from the wall, they heard a small, metallic clink.

Rodney looked under the dresser again, then he reached under and pulled out the watch.

"Voilà!" he cried. "The case of the missing wristwatch is solved, the innocent maid vindicated."

Mr. Stockwood looked behind the dresser.

"The baseboard stopped it from falling to the floor. But how did it get there?"

"Duchess," Aggie said, remembering. "She was on the dresser, looking at the birds when I came in with the vacuum cleaner."

"She hates the vacuum cleaner," Mrs. Bradley explained. "I bet she high-tailed it out of this room so fast the fur flew."

"The watch flew, in any case," Rodney said.

"My dear girl, I'm afraid we owe you an apology," Mrs. Stockwood said. "We should never have doubted your honesty."

"We certainly shouldn't have leapt to conclusions," Mr. Stockwood said. "If young Sherlock hadn't been home, I hate to think what might have happened. That watch would have stayed there until the next time the room was painted. I hope we can make this up to you, Agnes. You will stay with us, won't you?"

"I'll have to think about it, sir," Aggie said. "I'll talk to my sister tomorrow." Now that it was over, Aggie felt weak in the knees.

That evening, before Aggie went to sleep, there was a knock at her door. Mrs. Bradley came into her room. This had never happened before. She stood there awkwardly in her hairnet and housecoat, a tall, weathered-looking woman with large, red hands. Aggie wondered what she wanted. Suddenly, Mrs. Bradley pointed to the photograph on Aggie's bedside table. "Who are those children?" she asked.

"My wee brothers and sisters," Aggie said, and she found herself telling Mrs. Bradley of her family in Scotland for the first time.

Mrs. Bradley picked up the photograph.

"I wish I'd known that," she said. "I have a niece, you see, in Oshawa. Her husband ran off, left her with six children. I wanted Mrs. Stockwood to take on her oldest girl instead of you. Young Sarah's my godchild. She's a hard worker and I wanted her near me. I never had children of my own. Wilbert — that was my husband, Mr. Bradley — was killed in the war. Not the Great War, the Boer War, in Africa. He was twenty-two. We were married less than a year."

Mrs. Bradley sighed, but there was no self-pity in her voice. She might have been telling Aggie someone else's story, not her own.

"I've always been close to Sarah, but she's only fourteen and she's never worked outside her mother's house. Mrs. Stockwood wouldn't hear of it; had her heart set on a British domestic, just like all her friends. So when you came, I guess I blamed you. Over the past few weeks, watching you at spring cleaning, I realized I was probably wrong. Sarah's little more than a child. It'd be cruel to make her work as hard as you have.

"I know what might have happened if we'd branded you a thief. Mr. Stockwood was right; but for young Rodney, we'd have done a terrible wrong. You have every right to march out of this house. I'll give you a reference if you do. But, if you decide to stay, maybe we can start over. I'm not the best company, I know that, but perhaps we could be more civil with each other."

Aggie nodded.

"I'd like that," she said.

When Mrs. Bradley left the room, Aggie turned out her light and buried her face in her pillow. If Mr. Stockwood's watch had still been behind his dresser, she could not have cried harder.

Chapter Six

Rose

"You'll not stay another night in that house if I can help it!" Emma cried.

It was early Sunday afternoon and the two girls sat on a stone bench, part of a fountain in a little park on St. Clair Avenue near the Stockwood house. Aggie had just finished telling Emma the story of the wristwatch. The fountain only held a few dead leaves, but Toronto had opened to the spring like a flower in the sun. Children tumbled on the grass while automobiles motored by with the sunlight glinting off them. The sky above was a clear, gentle blue. To Aggie, it hardly seemed possible that this was the place she had spent the winter.

Emma was not always kind, but her anger comforted Aggie now. Aggie weighed her words carefully before replying.

"It was awful, Em, and I know I just escaped by the skin of my teeth. But they really are sorry — even Mrs. Bradley. I've worked so hard all these weeks, hoping things might be better. Now, if I stay, I think they will be. But if I leave, there's no promise I'd be treated better somewhere else."

Emma thought for a moment before nodding.

"If that's really what you want," she said at last. "But I'll try to have something lined up for you if you change your mind."

Aggie put her hand on her sister's arm.

"Thanks, Em. I think I'll be fine. If only..." she hesitated.

"If only what?" Emma asked.

"Well, there's Rodney. Remember what Molly said about university students? He seems nice enough, but now...well, I feel I owe him something."

Emma snorted. "Molly's a fool. It's true some girls aren't safe where they work, but you can always spot a man like that."

"You can?"

"Och, aye," Emma said. "The lads that are all leering eyes and big, rude mouths. They're the ones to watch. He hasn'a tried to touch you, has he?"

Aggie told her about the kiss on the hand.

Emma laughed.

"In front of Mrs. Bradley? And that was before he found the watch? Well, he sounds odd, but not the type to take advantage of you." Emma paused. "Watch out for his friends though. Lads can be dangerous when they group together. Just like wee children, they can egg one another on. Now," she rose from the bench, "we'd better go." She waved in the direction of the church across St. Clair Avenue. "It's so kind of the well-to-do to give us our afternoon service and a wee drop of tea. Who knows what mischief we might get up to otherwise? All the closed up shops might make burglars of us." She winked at Aggie, who laughed in spite of herself.

"Emma Maxwell, you've a hard heart. That 'wee drop of tea' saves us the price of a supper."

"It's true," Emma said. "They're generous enough with the food, but they do it to keep an eye on us all the same. They dinna trust us, Aggie. That's the truth. You saw that yourself this week."

As they set off for church together, Aggie had to admit that Emma was right. And, knowing that, perhaps she was wrong to be so trusting in return.

The sun was just setting when Aggie returned to the Stockwood house that evening. Daffodils nodded on the lawn, bright as lamps against the gathering darkness. Sunday dinner was always at noon. Mrs. Bradley took Sunday afternoons off as well. The evening meal was little more than a snack, the most informal meal of the week. So Aggie wasn't surprised to find Rodney in the kitchen, scrambling eggs. As usual, a book was never far from his side. One lay open on the table, waiting.

"Ah, Agnes," he said, "have you eaten?"

Aggie nodded.

"Perhaps you'd like a cup of tea?"

He seemed determined to make friends, and Aggie was grateful to him for finding the watch. So, even though she would have been happier to slip upstairs unnoticed, she poured herself a cup of tea and sat down.

Rodney joined her with his food.

"You spoke with your sister today?" he asked.

Aggie nodded again.

"Won't you tell me what you've decided?"

"Well, sir..."

"Rodney...please," Rodney interrupted her.

"...I've decided to stay," Aggie finished.

"Oh, I am pleased to hear that," he said. He looked pleased. "If you'd left we would have counted it a black mark against us."

"Well, if not for you, I'd be out of work without a reference by now. Thank you for your help," Aggie said.

"It was nothing really. You mustn't feel grateful. Actually, just this afternoon I was telling a friend what happened. We agreed it really would have been too terrible if you'd left. My friend would like to meet you."

"But why?" Aggie asked, amazed.

"Well, curiosity mainly," Rodney said. "We'll have lunch together some time this week. You can meet after."

Aggie remembered what Emma had said about young men in groups.

"I dinna think that would be proper."

Rodney dismissed her concern with a wave of his hand.

"Oh, proper...don't let that bother you. I insist."

As far as Rodney was concerned, the subject was closed. Aggie didn't see how she could possibly say more without embarrassing them both, so she finished her tea. She would have waited to wash Rodney's dishes, but he wouldn't hear of it.

"I'm certainly capable of washing a few dishes on a Sunday evening. Off you go," he said. Kind though he was, Aggie noticed he was certainly accustomed to getting his own way.

That night, Aggie dreamed she was in a motorcar with two young men. She had no idea where they were going but she was filled with dread. One of the young men said, "You haven't got a thing to worry about. Don't give it another thought," as the car hurtled on into the night. It was Rodney's voice, and it did not reassure her. Aggie woke up in the morning determined to spend no time with Rodney's friends.

Aggie spent most of Tuesday morning in the big, walk-in linen closet on the second floor. The winter blankets and bedding had been sent out to a laundry during spring cleaning. Now she packed them in mothballs for the summer. In that airless space she lost track of time, and Mrs. Bradley had to come and get her well after lunch. Aggie noticed that the sandwich Mrs. Bradley had made for her was more generous than usual. Meals had improved since their conversation in Aggie's bedroom.

"After you've eaten, you can take a tea tray into the sunroom. Rodney's friend would like to meet you."

Aggie's stomach lurched.

"Mrs. Bradley, does this not seem a bit...improper to you?" she asked.

"There's plenty improper about Rodney's friends, I'll tell you. But I don't imagine a few minutes will harm you. Rodney has his heart set on it," Mrs. Bradley added.

When Aggie finished her lunch, she took the tray to the bright glassed-in sunroom just off the sitting room. This room was too cold to be used in winter, but during spring cleaning Aggie had washed all the windows and carried in every plant in the house. It was lovely and, in spite of her apprehension, it pleased Aggie to be there. In any case, she was sure these young men would quickly tire of her company.

Rodney's friend was sitting in a big, wing-back chair facing away from Aggie. She put the tea tray down on the table before glancing quickly in that direction. What she saw surprised her so much she was glad she'd already put the tray down. There sat a girl about her own age. She was small, almost as small as Aggie herself, but softly plump. Her thick, chestnut-brown hair was short and curly. She had rosy cheeks, a small, upturned nose, and lively brown eyes.

"Agnes," Rodney said, "I would like you to meet my friend, Rose Chandler. Rose, this is Agnes Maxwell, of whom you have heard."

The girl named Rose smiled and pointed to a chair near her.

"Oh, please sit down. It'll be okay. Mrs. Stockwood's out and Rodney's good at getting what he wants from Mrs. Bradley." She laughed. Even though she was teasing Rodney, Aggie noticed there was no malice in her laughter.

Aggie glanced at Rodney who nodded, so she sat down.

Rose had been curled up in the big chair, but she unfolded now to pour tea. She was wearing a lovely, light blue frock and silk stockings. A rope of blue glass beads tinkled musically when she moved. She poured the tea with the careless grace of someone who had never once hurried to a command. She turned to Aggie as if she were a guest in the Stockwood house.

"Milk and sugar?" she asked.

Aggie glanced at Rodney again. Surely she could be let go for this. Rodney seemed to read her mind.

"Don't worry," he said, "Rose is right. Mrs. B. never gets angry with me."

"Neither does anyone else, Roddy," laughed Rose. "That's half the trouble." She handed Aggie a tea cup and turned to face her. "Rodney told me you came all the way from Scotland by yourself. Gee, that was brave. Was it exciting?"

Aggie remembered lying on the bunk in the cabin, sick for days.

"Not really, miss."

"Oh, can't you call me 'Rose'?" she asked. She made it sound as if Aggie would be doing her a favour. When Aggie hesitated, she said, "How old are you?"

"Seventeen, miss."

"Well, so am I. I don't like being called 'Miss Rose' by someone my own age."

Aggie wondered how she could make herself understood to this girl, who thought it would be exciting to come to Canada as a domestic.

"If I call you 'Rose' now, no one would mind. But if I forget, and call you 'Rose,' or call Mr. Rodney by his name in front of his parents, I might be in for trouble. Do you see?"

Rose laughed.

"Oh, we'd never let that happen, Agnes."

Aggie saw she could not make Rose understand. But it was so nice to be sitting in the sunroom instead of cleaning it. So pleasant to be holding one of Mrs. Stockwood's best cups filled with hot tea instead of warm dishwater. She silently forgave Rose and Rodney for the things they didn't know and could not even imagine about her life.

"Now, tell me about the watch," Rose said.

Aggie told the story, knowing that Rose had already heard it from Rodney. Nevertheless, Rose listened on the edge of her chair, giving Aggie her full and rapt attention.

"Just like something in a novel," she said when Aggie finished. "What a close call! I'd be furious if anything like that happened to me. Weren't you angry?"

Aggie shook her head.

"I might have been if I'd been sent away, but it happened so fast. After, I was only relieved."

"Well, that's because you're so sweet," Rose said. "Rodney told me you were."

Rose seemed to want to know everything about her. Aggie found herself speaking more freely even than she had with Emma's friends. She told Rose the story of Jen and Callum and the collection plate (leaving out the children's punishment, of course). Rose laughed and laughed, delighted as a child.

"It must be swell to have so many younger brothers and sisters," she said with a sigh. "I only have one older brother and he's as dull as dishwater."

"Your brother's going to be a very successful lawyer," Rodney said gently.

"See?" Rose said to Aggie. "What could be duller than that?"

When Aggie finally left the sunroom, she felt as if she had been on a holiday.

That evening, as Aggie was clearing away the supper dishes, she heard Mrs. Stockwood say to Rodney, "Was Rose Chandler over this afternoon?"

"Yes, Mother," Rodney replied.

"Back from her aunt's in Buffalo, is she?"

"Oh, so that's where Rose was," Mr. Stockwood said, "I wondered why we hadn't seen her before. She usually shows up a few minutes after Rodney arrives."

"Now, Father," Rodney said.

"Poor Rose," Mrs. Stockwood said. "You can't blame her for wanting to get away from her own house. When was the last time old Nate Chandler had a party? And that Bobby Chandler — I never met a duller young man."

"Nothing dull about Bobby," Mr. Stockwood said. "The boy's as sharp as a tack."

"Perhaps in the boardroom, dear," Mrs. Stockwood replied, "but not in the ballroom."

Aggie took the dishes into the kitchen, wondering how anyone could possibly feel sorry for Rose.

Now the house took on new life. Rose came almost every day. She listened to music on the Victrola with Rodney and they played croquet on the lawn, or sat reading books together. Rose devoured romance novels like candy. One day, while Aggie was dusting, she heard Rodney tease her about them.

"I could lend you a nice George Eliot, Rose. You don't have to read such trash. The slang you pick up from those romances makes you sound like a waitress sometimes." He tipped the book forward and read the title. "*Destiny's Desire*. It doesn't even make sense."

"It does too, Roddy. The main character is a girl named Destiny. I like romances. You always know there's going to be a happy ending, no matter how hard things seem. What's wrong with that?" Rose pushed her lower lip out like a child. Suddenly, she looked much younger than seventeen.

Rodney wasn't really capable of being angry.

"Nothing at all, I suppose," he said, and they went back to their books.

Rose seemed to take a special interest in Aggie. She always made a point of finding Aggie and talking to her for a few minutes. Unlike Emma's friends, she never tried to prove she knew more than Aggie did. Aggie began to look forward to seeing her.

Then, one Saturday morning, just as the weather turned hot, Rose came to play croquet. The big lawn at the back of the house was neatly mowed now by a gardener who came every week. Wire croquet hoops had been set out in a pattern under the trees, and Rodney and Rose spent hours knocking coloured wooden balls around with coloured wooden mallets. It seemed like a silly pastime to Aggie but they certainly enjoyed themselves. Their laughter often drifted in through the open windows.

Today Aggie sat at the dining room table, polishing the silver. Mrs. Stockwood had an endless store of silver and Aggie spent most of every Saturday morning polishing it.

She liked a job that let her sit down, but the blackened silver polish was messy. Today, the massive double doors between the dining room and the sitting room were open to let the air circulate. Mr. and Mrs. Stockwood sat in the sitting room, looking at magazines and newspapers, sometimes reading interesting bits aloud to one another. Aggie listened to them while she worked.

Suddenly, the swinging door to the kitchen burst open and there was Rose, breathless and laughing.

"Teddy Caldwell just came to play croquet, Mrs. Stockwood," she called into the sitting room, standing by Aggie. "No one else showed up. It'll be more fun if we play in pairs. Couldn't Agnes play, please?"

Aggie saw the look that Mr. and Mrs. Stockwood exchanged. This was an outrageous request.

"Oh, miss, that's not possible," Aggie said. She knew this was the right thing to say, but as she spoke she realized how much she longed to join the fun. She was sure there wasn't a hope, though.

Mr. Stockwood spoke. "Rose, I hardly know what to say..."

"Then just say yes, dear," Mrs. Stockwood said. "If it will make you happy, Rose."

Rose didn't give them a chance to change their minds. She snatched the polishing cloth from Aggie's hand and helped her to her feet.

"Come on, Agnes," she said, "that old silver will have to wait." And Rose hustled her into the kitchen.

"Wash those hands and get that apron off," Rose bossed Aggie as if she were talking to a child. This thought must have showed on Aggie's face. "I mean 'please'," Rose added hastily. "Oh, this is great! I've been trying to think of a way to get you out with us for weeks. This is swell!"

Aggie washed her hands, took off her headband and smoothed her hair. As she stepped out on the lawn, under the high green canopy of maples, she wished, just for a moment, that she could be wearing a pretty linen dress like Rose's instead of her drab, black uniform. But a fresh breeze took the heat from the air, and Aggie felt almost perfectly happy.

"Me and Teddy against you and Agnes," Rose said to Rodney.

"Do you know how to play?" Rodney asked.

Aggie shook her head.

"You're not likely to win, playing with me," she said.

"Rose has won already, as far as she's concerned," Rodney said. "Getting you out here was the object of her game. I didn't think she could. Now here's your mallet. Let me show you how to play."

Teddy Caldwell was a handsome boy, but painfully shy. He said practically nothing. In contrast, Rose and Rodney were like a couple of butterflies. They were everywhere. They knew the layout of the hoops (or wickets as Rodney called them) extremely well, and played hard. Aggie played badly at first, but halfway through the game she began to catch on. When she caught up with Rose, Rodney showed Aggie how to put her foot on the ball and hit it with her mallet, blasting Rose's ball under some shrubs and out of the game. Aggie was afraid Rose might be angry, but she just laughed. In the end, Aggie and Rodney won by a healthy margin.

"Your punishment," Rodney joked, "for recruiting Agnes away from the silver."

"Not on your life," Rose replied. "We haven't had this much fun all week."

Aggie glanced towards the house and saw Mrs. Bradley's face in the kitchen window.

"I really must get back to work now," she said. "It's almost time for lunch and the table's still covered in silver." She turned to Rodney. "Thank you," she said.

"Rosie engineered this, not me," Rodney said. "But I'm glad she did." And Aggie ran back to the house.

Mrs. Bradley looked so grim, Aggie was reminded of her first weeks in the Stockwood house.

"You'd better bring the silver in here" she said. Aggie obeyed. She settled down to work, rubbing harder than usual to make up for the time she'd missed. Mrs. Bradley's disapproval was palpable. Aggie waited for the lecture.

"It may be all right for Rodney and Rose, taking you away from your work, making you feel as if you're someone you can't be. But folks like us have got to know our place. Try to be someone you're not and no good will come of it," Mrs. Bradley said. To Aggie's surprise, there was no anger in her voice, just resignation, perhaps even concern.

"Now I'll set the table for lunch," Mrs. Bradley said, "seeing as how you're so far behind here." Setting the table was Aggie's job.

Aggie worked on the silver. The croquet game had been fun. Thursdays with Emma were not. When had Aggie last had fun? Maybe not since she'd come to Canada. What Mrs. Bradley said was true. Aggie worked hard, Rose never lifted a finger and that was that. No one would wave a magic wand and transform Aggie into a princess.

A burst of laughter carried in through the kitchen window. The blackened silver polish worked its way under Aggie's nails.

"I wish," she whispered under her breath, "that I could have some fun. I wish I was Rose." It seemed to Aggie that this wish, once spoken, should make her resent or dislike Rose. It didn't. Aggie knew that Rose would wish the same for her, if wishing helped. She sighed and gathered the silver for rinsing.

A few weeks later, Mrs. Bradley asked Aggie to get the suitcases out of Mr. and Mrs. Stockwoods' bedroom closet. "Just the two smaller ones. This is a weekend trip. They're going to Quebec City for their wedding anniversary."

"Oh, I remember Quebec City from the train. Will they stay in that castle?"

Mrs. Bradley laughed.

"If you mean the Chateau Frontenac, yes."

For the next week, Mrs. Stockwood was rarely seen without a hatbox or a dress in her hand. New gloves and shoes were ordered and the closet was emptied as she decided what could be packed and what would need to be replaced. There was lots of extra ironing to do.

Aggie heard Rodney complain one afternoon as she brought a tray of lemonade into the garden.

"Thank heaven Mother almost never travels. If this is a weekend in Quebec City, can you imagine what Europe would involve?"

Rose sat with her feet up, fanning herself ineffectually with a badminton racquet. The last time the lawn was mowed, Rodney and Rose had switched from croquet to badminton, which was all the rage this summer.

"Oh, lemonade. Thanks a million, Agnes." She took a frosted glass from Aggie's tray. "I think it's great that your mother's getting away," she said to Rodney. "Your father works too hard, just like my dad. They're so dull." Rose sighed. Then she sat up, suddenly alert. "How long will they be gone, Roddy?" she asked.

"Just Friday to Monday afternoon," Rodney said. "Rose, I know that look and it means trouble." He grinned. "I can almost hear the wheels going round. What's up?"

Aggie realized she'd probably stayed as long as she could. She started to turn back to the house, but Rose said, "No, Agnes, wait. There's a big dance at the Palais Royale Saturday night. Have you ever been there? Down at the Sunnyside Amusement Park?"

Aggie shook her head.

Rose leaned towards Rodney. Her eyes shone with excitement. She whispered loudly. "We have to take Agnes dancing Saturday night. We'll never have another chance like this. Oh Roddy, please?"

Aggie expected Rodney to nip the idea in the bud. Instead, he threw back his head and laughed.

"Rose, what a wicked idea."

To Aggie's surprise, she found her voice.

"But I canna go."

"And why not?" There was a dare in Rose's question. "Why shouldn't you have some fun? You're just as pretty and nice as any of the girls I know. But all you ever do is work. It's not fair. Oh, let us take you dancing, Agnes. It'll be so much fun."

"But I've no evening dress...I've no fancy shoes. And Mrs. Bradley will never approve," Aggie protested. But she wasn't serious. She was sure anyone could hear how much she really wanted to go.

"Just leave it to us," Rose said, dismissing Aggie with a wave of her hand. "Run along now before Mrs. B. wonders where you are."

Aggie turned back to the house. Once again, even though they were the same age, Rose had treated her as if she were a child. But Aggie hardly noticed. She had butterflies in her stomach, but at the same time she couldn't stop smiling. Rose was right. Why shouldn't Aggie have a little fun?

Mrs. Bradley noticed the smile.

"You look like the cat that swallowed the canary," she said as Aggie entered the kitchen. "What are those two up to out there?"

Aggie quickly tried to look more serious.

"Oh, nothing, Mrs. Bradley, nothing at all."

Now Mrs. Stockwood's excitement over the trip was mingled with the conspiracy to take Aggie dancing. The house, which had seemed so staid and dull to Aggie during the winter, was filled with an undercurrent of anticipation. The air almost crackled as Aggie flew through her chores with unusual energy.

Mrs. Bradley noticed.

"Agnes, these past few days I can scarcely find work enough for you. Rodney thought you might like this Saturday night out, with his parents gone and all, and I have to admit you won't be needed around here. Do you think you could stay out of mischief?" she asked.

"Oh aye, Mrs. Bradley," Aggie said, "I'm sure I could. Some of the girls my sister knows have their Saturday evenings now, with their employers gone on holiday and all." This wasn't a lie, but Aggie knew that Mrs. Bradley would assume she would be going out with those girls. That was almost lying. A little, niggling guilt tugged at Aggie's mind.

"Fine then. I'm sure I can trust a good girl like you. You know I like to go to bed right after my bath on Saturdays. I'll give you my keys if you promise to be careful with them."

Aggie nodded.

On Friday, Rodney drove his parents to Union Station and returned with the car. The next day, Rose came with a big canvas bag.

"I'll leave this in the hall closet. Take it up to your room as soon as you can," she hissed. "Be sure to take the dress out before it gets too wrinkled."

While Mrs. Bradley was making lunch Aggie took the bag upstairs. She could not suppress a cry of delight when she saw the dress. It was silvery blue, covered in sequins to the waist with a many-layered skirt of filmy chiffon. The neck was high enough in front, but the back was daringly low. Rose had thought of everything — a little blue evening bag, new silk stockings and even dancing shoes. Aggie hugged the dress and hung it on the back of the door. It was so beautiful, she was afraid it would shine with its own light and betray its presence.

After lunch that afternoon, Rose and Rodney got out the Victrola. Aggie tried to avoid the sitting room but was drawn to the doorway.

"Come on," Rose said grabbing her by the hand. "Can you tango?" Aggie shook her head. Except for Scottish country dancing at weddings, no one in Loughlinter danced. She'd only seen the tango at the pictures. "I'll teach you," Rose said.

Rodney laughed.

"Rosie likes to lead," he said. "I'm the only one who lets her."

Rose stuck out her tongue at Rodney, grabbed Aggie by the shoulder with one hand, and stuck their arms straight out on the other side.

"Together now, one, two, one, two, one, two and turn..."

Rodney picked the records and kept the Victrola cranked up. Rose was a good teacher. After the tango, they progressed to the foxtrot, and finally the Charleston.

Mrs. Bradley had decided to ignore them. She spent the afternoon reading magazines in the garden with her feet up. When they were danced out, Rodney and Rose went to the kitchen with Aggie and poured three glasses of buttermilk. They sat together and chatted like real friends.

"I've got to go," Rose said finally, rising. "Dad hates to eat alone and Bobby almost always works late. Even on the weekends."

"Do you want me to run you home, Rose?" Rodney asked.

"Thanks Rodney, but I'd rather walk. It only takes ten minutes. Now, the dancing doesn't start until ten. We can get something to eat first. When can you leave, do you think?"

"As soon as Mrs. Bradley's in the bathtub, Agnes can get dressed and leave without being seen. I'll take the car a while before. Agnes, you can meet me by that little park around the corner. Then we'll drive over and pick you up. Okay, Rose?"

"Sounds swell," Rose turned to Aggie. "Did you have a look at the dress?"

"It's beautiful," Aggie said.

"Bobby bought it for me last Christmas. It's so nice I didn't have the heart to tell him it was too tight on me. It should fit you perfectly. What size shoes do you take?" Rose asked.

"Five."

Rose's face fell.

"Oh no, I take an eight! You'll never be able to dance in my shoes. This is terrible."

"Where are we going to find size five shoes now?" Rodney asked.

Aggie knew she couldn't dance in shoes three sizes too big. She wouldn't really be able to walk in them. Her everyday shoes were old, thick-heeled and black — far too plain to wear with an evening dress. A disappointed silence filled the room.

Aggie knew it should end here, but she just couldn't give up the idea of the dance. Then she realized something.

"Your mother takes a size five shoe," she said to Rodney. "She gave me her old boots last winter."

"Brilliant!" cried Rodney. "Agnes saves the day. Shoes are a weakness with Mother. She has dozens. Go up and pick some out now," he said to Aggie.

Aggie's courage failed her.

"Oh, Rodney, I dinna dare. It's more than my job is worth."

"I'll do it," Rose said. "I'll just pretend I'm going to the bathroom. I'll leave them inside the door of your room, Agnes. Boy, that was close."

And she was gone.

The ordinary tasks of getting dinner ready and washing the dishes seemed to take forever that night. But the relaxed, holiday feeling persisted and Rodney insisted on drying the dishes. Finally, he looked at his watch.

"Rose will expect me soon." He lied with the air of someone practised in deception. "Time to change. Goodnight, Mrs. B. Goodnight, Agnes." He winked at her before he left the room.

"My old bones are weary tonight," Mrs. Bradley said. "I surely don't feel like someone who spent all afternoon lazing around. I can hardly wait to get into that bath." She suppressed a yawn. "Here are my keys. Now you be a good girl, Agnes. Stay with them other girls and don't go off with strangers. And make sure you get home before the streetcar stops running. I'll see you in the morning." And she went upstairs.

Rodney reappeared shortly, dressed to the nines, his thin blond hair slicked back on his head.

"The bath is running," he said. "When it stops you'll be safe to leave. I'll meet you." And he went whistling out the door.

When Aggie stood face to face with the dress alone, her heart pounded. But she could hear Mrs. Bradley splashing in the bathtub. It was almost too easy. She slipped out of the drab black uniform and the blue party dress shimmered over her shoulders. She spun around to make the short skirt fly. She felt like Cinderella. She took her plain cotton stockings off and slipped the new silk ones on. Then she noticed the shoes. They were blue kid shoes with thin straps and a tiny heel, elegant little shoes that looked as if they'd never been worn. They fit perfectly. Aggie combed out her hair, clipping it back on either side, but leaving it loose. She considered her reflection in the small, dark mirror. Everything was just right except — no jewellery. From the bedside table she took the marcasite swallow brooch that Davy had given her. She almost pinned it to the dress, but stopped. She put the brooch away. It wasn't good enough for this evening. Better to go without.

It was time. Aggie had to stop herself from tiptoeing down the stairs. She felt like a thief.

"All set to go?" Mrs. Bradley called from the bathroom.

Aggie resisted the urge to bolt down the stairs.

"Yes, Mrs. Bradley," she replied in the calmest voice she could find.

"Don't forget to lock the door."

"I won't," Aggie replied. She looked up and down the hall, hesitating for just a moment. Then she turned away from the gloomy servants' stairs, walked down the mahogany staircase, past the beautiful stained glass window and out the front door. As she stepped into the street, a cool breeze stirred against her skin.

Chapter Seven

The Palais Royale

"Shrimp cocktails." Rose addressed the waiter with authority. "And ginger ale...oh, in champagne glasses, please." The waiter smiled in spite of Rose's bossy tone, nodded and left. Rose sighed. "Wouldn't it be great to be twenty-one and drink real champagne?" she said.

"Just as well you two are underage," Rodney replied. "I have a feeling you'll be enough of a handful for me tonight dead sober."

Rose giggled. She was wearing a satin dress of deep, lustrous pink with a long rope of pearls around her neck. A kiss curl had been brought down to the middle of her forehead for the evening. She was wearing lipstick and maybe even a little rouge. Aggie thought she looked like the perfect flapper.

They were sitting in the restaurant of the King Edward Hotel, an elegant room with lofty windows and elaborate plaster mouldings. Aggie had spent the first few minutes staring directly at the water glass beside her plate. She couldn't shake the feeling someone was going to recognize her and ask her to leave. Now that the waiter had taken their order, she began to relax.

The shrimp cocktails arrived and so did the ginger ale. The waiter had thoughtfully wrapped the bottle in a towel and placed it in an ice bucket, playing along with Rose's fantasy of champagne. So this is what it's like, Aggie thought. Everything just the way you want it, just because of who you are. Rodney filled the three champagne glasses and Rose proposed a toast.

"To Agnes Maxwell, our visitor from Scotland," she said just loudly enough so people at the tables around them smiled and nodded in Aggie's direction.

"To Agnes," Rodney chimed in.

Suddenly Rose let out a high-pitched squeak. At first, Aggie thought she was choking. But the squeak sounded like a word. Aggie realized the word was "Bobby!" Rose was not choking, but she was looking towards the door.

Rodney followed Rose's gaze.

"That is indeed your brother Bobby, the boring lawyer, as you style him. I do believe he's noticed us as well."

Aggie thought Rose would hide under the table.

"He's coming this way! What'll we do?" she said in a hoarse whisper.

Rodney gripped her elbow briefly.

"Steady on, Rosie. We're just showing my cousin from Scotland the sights. Where's the harm in that?"

If Aggie had imagined Bobby Chandler at all, she saw him as a thin, pale soul bent over his law books in an airless office. But the young man striding towards them now was certainly Rose's brother. He had the same thick chestnut hair and laughing brown eyes. He was short, like Rose, and not thin, but his stockiness gave him a muscular look. If not for his evening clothes, he might have just stepped out of a forest or off a sailboat. He looked directly at Aggie, nodded to Rodney, then turned to Rose.

"So here you are. Father told me you were out for the evening. I was supposed to meet my stockbroker for dinner, but there was a message at the desk saying he'd couldn't make it. You don't mind if I join you, do you? I'm starved."

For the first time since Aggie had known her, Rose was speechless. Rodney spoke up quickly.

"Certainly not, although I'm sure you'll find us rather frivolous compared to your stockbroker. Bobby, I'd like you to meet my cousin Agnes Maxwell, who is visiting from Scotland."

The waiter brought another chair and Bobby sat beside Aggie.

"I've always wanted to visit Scotland. Do you live in Edinburgh?"

"No...Glasgow," Aggie said.

"I see. Will you be visiting long?" Aggie noticed that, like Rose, Bobby gave the person he spoke to his full attention. It was very flattering. So much so that it took her a moment to realize he was waiting for an answer she didn't have.

"Sadly no," Rodney said, filling in the pause. "I'm afraid Agnes and her parents are planning to spend most of their time with my sister Linda. They take the train to Regina on Monday."

Just then the waiter arrived and Bobby ordered his dinner.

As they ate and chatted, Bobby asked Aggie all about Scotland. It wasn't difficult for Aggie to describe places she'd only seen in newspapers and magazines, especially as none of the others seemed to know much about her country.

"What a pity you're leaving so soon," Bobby said as he finished his dinner. "We could have shown you around Toronto...couldn't we, Rose?"

"Well, we are, tonight," Rose replied. "We're taking Agnes to dance at the Palais Royale. I'm sure you have better things to do."

Bobby smiled at Aggie.

"Not at all. I can't remember the last time I went dancing." He turned to Rodney. "You don't mind if we make it a foursome, do you, Stockwood?"

"No," Rodney said. But his voice went up, so that it sounded more like a question than an answer.

"That's settled then," Bobby said. It occurred to Aggie that she had just met someone who was even better at getting his own way than Rodney was.

"I'm going to powder my nose before we move on," Rose said. "Agnes, why don't you come with me?"

As soon as they passed through the swinging door of the powder room, Rose turned and grabbed Aggie by the elbows.

"Bobby never comes anywhere with us. He thinks Rodney is a fool. He thinks I'm a baby. I can't believe this."

Aggie gave a shaky laugh.

"We've done pretty well so far, I think."

"Pretty well? Agnes, you were brilliant. How much of that stuff was made up?"

"Quite a bit," Aggie admitted. "I've never even been to Edinburgh, or the Isle of Skye."

"Well, I'd never have guessed." Rose sat down on a plush chair and began to pull a comb furiously through her thick hair. "You know what I think? I think Bobby is stuck on you."

Standing behind Rose, Aggie watched herself turn bright red in the mirror.

"Oh, Rose, that canna be."

"No, really. He certainly isn't hanging around to be with Rodney. Or me." She opened her lipstick, then paused. "What if he fell in love with you? What if he married you? Just like a romance novel. Then you wouldn't have to work. We'd be sisters." She took out a compact and began to powder her face.

Just for a moment, Aggie imagined it. Then she forced herself back to reality.

"Things like that dinna happen," she said.

"Oh, sure they do! I read a story just like that in *Chatelaine* last month. A rich young heir married his secretary. I bet it happens every day."

Aggie knew there was no point in telling Rose that a secretary was not a domestic. Rose saw everything through such a haze of romance that those distinctions were too fine for her.

Rose snapped her compact shut and turned to face Aggie.

"I know Bobby and one thing's for sure: he thinks you're terrific."

Rodney and Bobby were waiting in the lobby.

"That's a lovely dress you're wearing, Agnes," Bobby said as they started towards the door. "Don't you have one something like that, Rose?"

Rose didn't miss a beat.

"Yes, Bobby, dresses like that are all the rage this year." She winked at Aggie when her brother wasn't looking.

The Palais Royale was right down on the lake. A breeze off the water cooled the air. But inside, the dance hall was hot, smoky, and crowded. The hot jazz, the smoke, the young men and women in their evening clothes, all made Aggie's head spin. She'd never seen anything like this. But she soon discovered that Bobby hadn't been lying about not being able to remember the last time he went dancing. He barely knew the steps. Rodney took pity on Aggie after a while and asked her to dance.

"You seem to have made a conquest," he said.

"Oh, dinna be daft," Aggie said. She had almost forgotten that Rodney was her employers' son.

"I'm serious. Bobby never goes out. He's a very good lawyer, though," Rodney said. "My father has nothing but praise for him."

"Well, I'm glad he didn'a try to make a living as a dancer," Aggie said. "He'd have starved to death. I'm terrified he's going to step on your mother's shoes."

"And other than that?" Rodney probed gently.

"Well, he's perfect. Just like Rose. But dinna forget, I'm taking the train to Regina on Monday."

Rodney laughed.

When they went back to the table, Rodney said, "It's far too hot in here. Perhaps Agnes would like to see the lake."

"That would be lovely," Aggie said, giving Rodney a grateful look. Outside, shrieks and laughter from the amusement park across the street mingled with the fading music from the Palais. The night air was filled with the smells of frying doughnuts and redhots.

"We'll walk towards the bathing pavilion," Bobby said.

He took the lead with Aggie purposefully, leaving Rodney and Rose behind. Out beyond the breakwater, a thin crescent moon cast a ladder of silver light across the lake. Aggie still felt giddy. Along the boardwalk, they passed something like a stage that enclosed a large machine.

"'Auditorium Orthophonic Victrola,'" Aggie read. "What is that?"

"It's the largest Victrola in the world," Bobby said. "Nine feet high. They say you can hear the music over a mile away."

Aggie gazed at it for a moment, then looked around. Sunnyside was full of light and sound and colour on this hot summer evening.

"You have a very beautiful city, Mr. Chandler," Aggie said. She had almost forgotten she wasn't a visitor from Scotland.

"Then you must visit more often. But please...everyone calls me Bobby — although I'm beginning to feel it's a little childish. Perhaps you could too."

Aggie nodded.

"Your sister Rose is lovely," she said.

"My sister Rose is a child." Bobby waved his hand dismissively towards the couple behind them. "It's kind of your cousin to spend so much time with her. My mother died when Rose was quite young. My father's on the same board of directors as your uncle. That's how we know your family. I'm with a small law firm. My father and I both work hard. I'm afraid our household is very dull for Rose. I've spoken to Father about allowing Rose to travel, or perhaps to attend the university. Lots of girls from good families take classes these days. But he has old-fashioned ideas about women and their place. Rose is to run his house until she marries. He sees that as her only proper work. Are your parents more liberal?"

"No, my parents are quite old-fashioned too," Aggie said.

Rose and Rodney joined them just in time to hear Bobby's next question.

"And what does your father do?" he asked.

"Agnes's father is involved in coal mining concerns," Rose said quickly. "That's right, isn't it?" She smiled at Aggie.

"Aye," was all that Aggie could manage to say.

"Really?" Bobby said. His interest seemed sparked. "The coal mining industry is quite depressed these days. I have some mining investments of my own. I don't suppose I could talk to your father before you leave?" he asked.

Aggie almost panicked. Rodney came to the rescue.

"I'm afraid my aunt and uncle went away with my parents this weekend. My parents planned the trip a long time ago — it's their wedding anniversary. Agnes was too tired to make the extra journey and decided to remain here. They'll only be back briefly before the train leaves for Regina. I am sorry. Now, the traffic will be terrible when the dance is over. Let's get away."

Bobby hesitated.

"Perhaps, Agnes, you and Rodney would join Rose and me for tea tomorrow afternoon. We could take the ferry to the island. There's quite a view of the city from there."

Rodney started to speak, but Aggie was quicker.

"That would be lovely," she said. "What time?"

When they dropped Rose and Bobby off, the night had finally cooled. A light breeze whispered through the trees as they drove home. The streets were empty.

"So, our little sparrow turns into a goldfinch," Rodney teased her. "I wonder, though, is it wise to see Bobby again?"

"Oh, Rodney, none of this is wise. It's just...well, I've one good dress, an afternoon dress, that I could wear to a fancy tea. And I'm tired of spending my Sunday afternoons at the domestics' church service. I couldn'a resist. And Bobby seems to need someone to talk to. He told me all about his family," she said. "He made it sound very dull."

Rodney nodded.

"I think Bobby is lonely. And you're right. Their life is dull. Especially for Rose. That's why she spends so much time at our house. What Bobby probably didn't tell you is that their father restricts Rose terribly. He trusts me, because he's known me all my life. But he rarely lets Rose out with anyone else. It's a very artificial situation. And it works to keep Rose a child. No wonder she reads all those romance novels. I can't imagine how she's supposed to meet a husband. I suppose he really doesn't want her to."

Aggie sat for a minute in stunned silence. At any other time she would not have been so bold, but tonight everything was different.

"You mean...but I thought..." she faltered.

"...that I was courting Rose?" Rodney finished the sentence for her. He sighed. "I suppose that's what everyone thinks. Rose knows we're only friends, of course. My parents hope I'll settle down soon. But I have ambitions, Agnes. Not like everyone else. I don't want to make a killing on the stock market or run a bank. The past is the only thing I've ever taken seriously. I want to do advanced degrees in history. That's why people like Bobby Chandler think I'm a fool. There's no money in it.

"I know what I want, but I also know I'll be poor for a long time to come. Maybe forever. It would be wrong to marry until I know I can earn a living. Still, someone with my background looks pretty appealing to the young debutantes of this city — and their mothers. I used to have a hard time keeping out of their way. I didn't start spending time with Rose to stop that, of course. I'm fond of her and she needs a friend. But I've discovered that Rose does an excellent job of keeping other young ladies away. And I make sure Rose gets out. It's not a perfect arrangement, but it suits us."

They pulled into the Stockwood driveway. Rodney put his finger to his lips.

"Mrs. B. must be sound asleep by now, but I'll go in the back way just to make sure the coast is clear," he whispered.

"I'll wave a dishtowel out the back door when I'm sure it's safe. Watch for me."

Aggie sat alone in the car, looking down at the shimmering dress Bobby had given his sister Rose. Just a few hours ago, Aggie would willingly have traded places with Rose, the princess with the perfect wardrobe, the perfect beau, the perfect life. Now, it felt good to be Aggie, waiting for the dishtowel signal that would let her back into her mousey life.

Mousey until tomorrow, she thought as the dishtowel appeared.

Chapter Eight

Japanese Lanterns

Sunday afternoon was bright and sunny. Aggie had no trouble pretending she was going to the domestics' church service. She didn't even have to worry about Emma, because Emma had a boyfriend now and almost always spent Sunday afternoons with him. Aggie was glad of that for another reason: she couldn't imagine what Emma would say if she knew Aggie was going to dances and teas with her employers' son.

After lunch, Aggie slipped upstairs. The blue kid evening shoes Rose had picked for her yesterday would not do for afternoon. She quietly crept to Mrs. Stockwood's closet and traded them, being careful to take an older-looking pair this time. Just yesterday, "borrowing" shoes from Mrs. Stockwood's closet was unthinkable. She slipped the shoes to Rodney. He would hide them in the car so Aggie would be able to change out of her old shoes on the way to the ferry docks. Aggie dressed quickly. In the navy silk dress Mrs. MacDougall had given her, she could almost believe she *was* an heiress from Scotland. Rodney waited in the car by the little park around the corner, just as he had the night before.

Aggie had visited Toronto Island with Emma, who liked Hanlan's Point with its amusement park and bandstand. Centre Island had summer hotels and picnic grounds. It was more sedate — not to Emma's liking, so Aggie had only been there once.

"We'll go to Centre Island," Bobby said as they met at the foot of York Street. "Hanlan's is so crass." The island shimmered out on the lake as they boarded the *Trillium*.

Aggie liked the tubby ferries with their black wooden hulls and flower names: the *Primrose*, the *Bluebell*, the *Mayflower* and the *Trillium*. Out on the water, the sturdy *John Hanlan* came towards them, heading from the island to the city. The *Hanlan* was a smaller boat, sharp-prowed and graceless. Black smoke poured from her funnel. She made the bigger ferries seem like fat, contented swans.

"Oh, the *Hanlan*," Rodney said. "They're taking it out of service soon."

Bobby looked at him with curiosity.

"How on earth do you know that?"

"I read it in the paper."

"Roddy remembers everything," Rose said.

"What will happen to that boat?" Aggie asked. She couldn't say so now, of course, but the *Hanlan* was the first ferry she'd taken to the island. She was fond of the homely old boat.

No one had any idea. As the *Hanlan* passed, Aggie thought: everyone in Canada is in such a hurry to leave the past behind. No one wants the old things. And she silently wished the *Hanlan* goodbye.

When Aggie and Emma came to the island, they always brought their own lunch, usually a bunch of bananas purchased at a city fruit stand for a nickel, eaten on a park bench.

Now, as the *Trillium* slipped back towards the city, Bobby led the way to Manitou Road on the far side of the island.

"I think we'll go to Gin's Casino," he said.

Aggie stopped dead in confusion. Gin's Casino sounded like a speakeasy, a place where people would gamble and drink hard liquor.

"I dinna think..." she began, her voice trailing off.

Rose looked at her with concern for an instant and then laughed.

"Oh, Agnes, Gin's is just a restaurant with a dance floor. They don't have a liquor license or anything."

"They do have the best ice cream on the island, though," Bobby said. As Rose and Rodney went ahead he added, "I'm sorry Agnes. I wouldn't have alarmed you for anything in the world."

Manitou Road, the main street of Centre Island, was so busy it seemed like the heart of a small town. The restaurant overlooked the dance floor — empty of course. There was no dancing on Sundays.

Rose wore a pale blue linen suit, her rope of pearls, blue lace gloves, and a broad-brimmed straw hat that almost covered her face completely. Aggie had no summer gloves. The hat she wore to church was so shabby she'd left it in the car with her old shoes. Looking at Rose, she realized that her one good dress, even the borrowed shoes and stockings were not enough. Pretending to be something I'm not is hard, she realized, almost impossible. How could I keep up with Rose? I'm glad, Aggie thought, that this will be the last day of pretending — well, almost glad. It was hard to feel happy about the black uniform and mountains of laundry that were waiting for her tomorrow.

After tea, they walked back to view the city skyline. Bobby took Aggie's elbow as they walked across the grass, just as Davy used to in Scotland. The harbour shimmered blue and cool between the island and the hot city. Bobby pointed to the tallest building on the skyline, still no more than a tower of raw steel girders, half clad in stone.

"That new skyscraper is going to be the Royal York Hotel," Bobby said. He sounded as if he owned it himself. Aggie remembered how the skeleton of the Royal York had greeted her when she stepped out of Union Station with Emma.

"You seem very proud of it," she said.

Bobby nodded.

"I'm proud of the whole country. Every bit of it. The Great War is behind us. We have nothing but peace and prosperity to look forward to. With hard work and ambition, any man can make his fortune in Canada." He smiled at her. "Will you pass through Toronto again on your way home?"

Rodney, who was standing nearby, overheard and spoke up quickly.

"I'm afraid Agnes will take the train straight through to Montreal on the return trip. Won't you, Agnes?"

Aggie realized that Rodney had decided the game had gone far enough.

"Oh, aye, we've some friends in Montreal who'd like to see us before we sail," she improvised.

"But surely you could stop over in Toronto just for a day or two," Bobby said. His distress was obvious.

"The tickets are purchased," Rodney said, "and we must avoid hurting anyone's feelings." He looked pointedly at Aggie.

"That's true," Aggie agreed. "If I were to change my plans now, feelings would certainly be hurt."

Bobby didn't try to hide his disappointment. Aggie realized that Rose was not simply imagining things. Bobby did care for her, or at least for the wealthy young visitor from Scotland that she seemed to be. As they went towards the ferry dock to go home, Bobby slipped a small card to Aggie.

"My address," he said. "Perhaps you'll write to me."

Aggie stared at the card, not knowing what to say. She was as fond of Bobby Chandler as she'd ever been of any young man. But how could she agree to write from a place she wouldn't be? She looked up at Bobby. He blushed.

"Yes, well," he said, "I understand how busy your life must be." He turned away quickly. Aggie realized that Rodney might be too late in his bid to prevent hurt feelings.

Later, as they were stepping off the ferry in the city, Aggie caught the heel of Mrs. Stockwood's shoe in a space between the boat and the ramp. She pitched forward, almost falling, and the heel broke off.

"Oh no," cried Aggie, horrified. She could lose her job for this.

Bobby look puzzled.

"It's only a shoe," he said, then added, "Oh, I see, you're worried about leaving tomorrow. Well, there's a shoemaker in Union Station. I'm sure he'd be able to take care of it for you before you board your train."

Rodney picked up the heel and pocketed it.

"Don't worry Agnes, I'll see that it's fixed before it's needed again." And he helped Aggie limp to the car.

Aggie looked back over her shoulder at Bobby and Rose. In her panic, she hadn't said a proper goodbye. Bobby met her eyes briefly with his direct, open gaze. Then he looked away without attempting a polite smile. He took Rose by the arm and they turned towards their car. Just before they did, Rose winked at Aggie, but suddenly none of it seemed like a joke any more. The afternoon sun was oppressively hot. The shoe that had not broken had given Aggie a blister and worn a hole in one of the lovely silk stockings.

The shoes were still missing on Monday afternoon when Mrs. Stockwood burst in though the front door.

"Home again. Oh, isn't it lovely to be back?" she cried. Aggie came into the hall, willing herself to think of anything but shoes. Rodney followed his mother with the suitcases. His father had taken a taxi directly to his office.

"Really, Mother, anyone would think you'd been gone for weeks," Rodney joked.

"Well, it felt like weeks. Please take the bags upstairs, Rodney. I'm so hot and tired. What I need is a nice bath. Agnes, please unpack for me."

Aggie followed Rodney and his mother up the lovely staircase. She was wearing her drab black uniform again. To Aggie as well it seemed impossible that only three days had passed since the Stockwoods left. The shimmering evening dress was packed in Rose's canvas bag again, waiting for the moment when Aggie could slip it back to her. The enchanted weekend was over. Once again, Aggie was working hard to make other peoples' lives easier.

As Aggie unpacked Mrs. Stockwood's clothes, she tried to avoid looking at the closet floor, where dozens of shoes were lined up neatly. She felt a bit like a murderer at the scene of the crime. Rodney had taken the shoe to be repaired early that morning, as soon as he could. He was certain he would be able slip the pair into the closet before his mother noticed. Aggie was not so sure. Every time she thought about it, her heart pounded. This will be my punishment, she thought, for leading Bobby Chandler on.

Downstairs, the front doorbell rang. Before she could leave the bedroom, she heard Rodney say, "I'll get it." When

Aggie reached the top of the stairs, she saw Rodney holding a large paper cone that looked like flowers. He quickly reached inside, found a small card, glanced at it and tucked it into his pocket.

"Was someone at the door?" Mrs. Stockwood came out of the bathroom in her pink silk robe and padded over beside Aggie.

"Yes, Mother. Florist," Rodney said. Aggie noticed he had turned bright pink.

"Oh, how lovely!" Mrs. Stockwood hurried down the stairs. "Who could they be from? Find the card. There must be a card."

Rodney helped his mother tear the paper away from the flowers—pink lilies and salmon-coloured gladioli. Of course there was no card.

"Isn't that odd," Mrs. Stockwood said when they'd finished searching. "Perhaps I should call the florist."

"I'm sure they're for your wedding anniversary," Rodney said quickly.

"Oh, of course, they must. But who sent them? And why isn't there a card?"

"Perhaps the card was lost in transit. Linda must have had them sent, don't you think?"

Aggie knew Mrs. Stockwood could not imagine Rodney would ever mislead her.

"Yes," she said, "you must be right. Now look at me, in my dressing gown in the middle of the day. I'd better get dressed." And she padded back upstairs. "Just put those on the dining room table, would you, Rodney?"

"I've finished unpacking, Mrs. Stockwood," Aggie said when Mrs. Stockwood reached the top of the stairs.

"Oh fine, dear. That will be all for now."

As soon as his mother was out of sight, Rodney jerked his head towards the dining room, then disappeared with the flowers. Aggie followed.

"These," he whispered, pointing towards the flowers now on the dining room table, "are actually for you." He extracted a small card from his pocket. "Miss Agnes Maxwell" was inscribed on the envelope. Aggie opened it.

"'Bon voyage,'" she read, "'from your new Canadian friend, Bobby.' Oh dear."

"Oh dear, indeed. We let this go too far. If mother or Mrs. B. had opened that door, we'd both be in hot water and you might be out of a job."

Aggie looked at the flowers. No one had ever sent her flowers, and these were the most beautiful ones she'd ever seen.

"I feel terrible," she said. "It was so thoughtful of Bobby."

"You ought to be thinking of yourself, Agnes, not Bobby. We still have to get those shoes back into Mother's closet. Bobby will survive. We had no way of knowing this would happen. We were just going to a dance. The main thing is to make sure he never finds out. I'm sure mother won't suspect a thing if you just act normal."

Aggie tried to follow Rodney's advice, but she kept the card in her uniform pocket and went into the dining room whenever she could. Flowers for me, she chanted silently to herself as she worked, flowers for me.

Rodney told Rose, who had to see the flowers. Rodney and Aggie managed a moment when Mrs. Stockwood, still tired from the trip, was napping, and Mrs. Bradley was busy with the gardener outside.

"Oh, it's so romantic!" Rose said, touching the petals of a lily. "I didn't know Bobby had a romantic bone in his body. Roddy, why don't we tell him?"

"What!" Rodney was so loud that Aggie was afraid his mother might hear.

"No, really. He's obviously in love with Agnes. He'd come in here and sweep her off her feet. They'd get married and live happily ever after."

Rodney looked more serious than Aggie had ever seen him. He ran a hand though his thinning blond hair.

"Rose," he said, "this is not a romance novel. This is Toronto. This is 1928. Bobby thought Agnes was a young woman of good family, of money. Young lawyers do not marry domestic servants. I'm sorry, it just isn't done."

Rose looked disappointed, but she didn't argue. And although Aggie felt her cheeks burn, she knew Rodney was right.

In her room that night, Aggie held the two cards in her hands, the one Bobby had given her on the island, and the one that came with the flowers. The flowers themselves would be gone soon. Rodney was right, of course. Bobby Chandler would not fall in love with a domestic. But what if he had already fallen in love and then found out...She shook her head. I'll soon be as daft as Rose, she thought.

The next morning, Rodney was off early for tennis, before the courts became unbearably hot. It was almost lunchtime when Mrs. Stockwood called Aggie to her bedroom.

"Agnes," she said, "when you were unpacking did you see my navy shoes? The ones with the two thin straps and the little gold buckles?"

Aggie's heart began to pound. "Not while I was unpacking, Mrs. Stockwood," she said, truthfully. "Did you take them to Quebec?"

"No, I don't believe I did. They ought to be here somewhere. Perhaps you could help me look."

Aggie did, feeling more guilty by the moment. She hadn't seen Rodney before he left that morning to remind him to pick up the missing shoe. What if he forgot?

Aggie was beginning to wonder if it wouldn't be better to confess when Rodney passed the bedroom door a few minutes later, still dressed in his tennis whites.

"Anything wrong?" he asked.

Mrs. Stockwood told him. Aggie held her breath.

"Oh," Rodney said, "I believe I saw shoes like that in the hall closet this morning when I took my racquet out. Could they be there?"

"Well, I suppose. Agnes, please check for me. I'd like to wear those shoes this afternoon."

Aggie found the shoes just where Rodney had left them. It was impossible to tell the heel had been repaired. A wave of relief swept over her. I dinna deserve to get off like this, she thought. But she had.

The blast furnace heat of July gave way to the cooler clarity of August. Summer was almost over, and Aggie began to realize how much she would miss Rodney when he returned to Queen's. Rose's visits would stop then too. And what would she do without Rose? Now, as Aggie went about her work, she listened for the sound of their laughter, not with envy as she had at the beginning of the summer, but with a sense of longing and loss. She tried never to think about Bobby. But sometimes, in her dreams, she found herself walking by Lake Ontario, looking out over the moon-lit water, or back at the shimmering city. The attentive young man at her side was always Bobby. She never saw his face, and they never spoke. He was simply a solid presence at her side, someone to depend on. These dreams stayed with her, creating a kind of fog that comforted her and kept her from thinking too much about what might have happened — and what would not.

She caught herself staring off into space when she should have been working, and more than once she came into a room, knowing there was a reason for being there, but unable to remember it. Mrs. Bradley was right about knowing your place, Aggie told herself. Perhaps it would be better to spend more time with Emma. But Aggie didn't want to deal with Emma, or the new boyfriend Aggie had never met. With Emma, she could only be Aggie Maxwell, a domestic servant. Aggie would rather cling to the magic of that weekend when she had been someone else.

Before Rodney returned to Queen's, the house erupted in a small frenzy of activity. Just the perfect argyle socks must be found to match Rodney's new navy blazer, and dozens of white linen handkerchiefs, monographed with "RS" were necessary, apparently, for success at university. Then of course there were the truly important matters: winter coats (two) with matching gloves, hats and scarves. And boots so strong and finely made that toes could pass the winter in them without ever feeling cold. Rodney stood at the centre of all the fuss like the calm eye of a storm, tolerating it for the sake of his mother and Mrs. Bradley. It was not unlike the bustle before his arrival in the spring, but now Aggie understood why. How could anyone not like Rodney? When she compared her faded image of the stuffy, spoiled young man she had expected with the Rodney she had come to know, she was amazed that anyone could be so wrong. And she knew she would miss him.

Rose participated in the selection of winter clothes, but Aggie could see her heart wasn't in it. One afternoon, when Rodney had been called away to express his opinion on neckties, Rose lay across an easy chair in the sitting room with a shoe dangling from one foot, while she flipped list-lessly through a winter catalogue. Aggie was supposed to be ironing. Instead, she stayed. She hadn't had a chance to talk to Rose alone since the flowers came.

"I dread this fall," Rose said to Aggie. Then she bright-ened a bit. "Bobby promised to take me out more often, though, now that I'm almost eighteen. I hope he means it."

"How is Bobby?" Aggie asked, trying to keep her voice even.

Rose sat up.

"He still looks at the mail, first thing every night when he comes home. He still looks disappointed, every single night. And sometimes he asks, ever so casually, if Rodney ever hears from that charming cousin of his in Scotland."

Aggie knew she was blushing. She didn't care.

"What do you say?"

"I tell him that Agnes is known to be terrible about letters, that Rodney says she almost never writes anyone. Oh, Agnes, I really wish you could see him. If you were together again, I'm sure it would work out. He's really got it bad."

Rodney entered at that moment.

"Someone sick?" he asked.

"Housekeeper's son has the chicken pox," Rose said smoothly. She held up the catalogue. "How do you feel about these cufflinks, Roddy?"

Aggie remembered the ironing.

Later that afternoon, Aggie sat in the kitchen with a cup of tea while Mrs. Bradley worked on the grocery order.

"Olives, pickled onions...lots of extras this week," she said, "The missus has her heart set on giving Rodney a big send-off Saturday night. I'll teach you how to make those pinwheel sandwiches if you like. We'll be up to our ears in fancy tidbits for the next few days."

Aggie smiled.

"I'd like that."

Mrs. Bradley sighed.

"This place sure will be quiet with Rodney gone again. Seems the summer went by so quickly. Oh well, he'll be home at Christmas. Perhaps that won't seem too long."

The party made so much work that it was easy for Aggie to forget everything else for a few days. When she wasn't helping Mrs. Bradley, she was busy with cleaning that hadn't been done since spring. By Saturday, everything was perfect — except the weather. It was hot again, as hot as July. Mrs. Stockwood decided to have the party outside. In the afternoon, Aggie helped Rodney and Rose take down the badminton net and string Japanese lanterns across the garden. They seemed almost impossible to untangle, but at last the garden was crisscrossed with delicate paper globes.

Rose ran her arm over her forehead as she climbed down from the ladder.

"Whew, it's hot. Is that the last of them, Roddy?"

"I'm not sure," Rodney said, "I'll check the loft in the garage."

As soon as he disappeared, Rose whispered to Aggie, "I've got a surprise tonight. Wait and see."

She must have a going away present for Rodney, Aggie thought. Then Rodney emerged from the garage with another tangled mass of lanterns.

"Oh no," Rose groaned, and they set to work again.

By evening, sheet lightning flashed behind low clouds.

"I do hope it doesn't rain," Mrs. Stockwood said.

"Now dear," Rodney's father said, "you know sheet lightning doesn't always mean rain. Let's get those lanterns lit. If it starts to rain, we'll just move everything inside."

Aggie changed into a fresh uniform before the party started. Her little attic room was stifling, but through her tiny window the garden was transformed. Pink and green and blue and orange paper lanterns glowed softly, perfectly still in the hot night air. Gradually, the garden began to fill with guests.

"Real champagne!" Rose said as she slipped into the kitchen. "This is swell."

Aggie was filling a tray of flute glasses with champagne.

"This is perfect," Rose said. "It couldn't be better. Will you bring that tray into the garden when it's full?" Aggie nodded. "Terrific. See you out there."

And she was gone with a swish of her electric blue evening gown.

The sheet lightning flashed again as Aggie carefully swung the screen door open and, balancing the silver tray, stepped out into the night. The air hit her like something damp and solid. So many people were in the garden now she couldn't tell who was there. The Japanese lanterns cast a gentle glow over everything. Rodney approached, looking surprisingly serious. "Agnes," he said, "could I have a word with you?"

"As soon as I finish with this tray..." Aggie started to say, but Rodney's friends came for him before she could finish. He glanced back anxiously as he was spirited away. Aggie could barely see Rose in one of the few chairs, facing some young men who stood with their backs to the house. Rose, Aggie knew, would want champagne, and tonight she would have a glass. Aggie made her way through the crowd, stopping whenever she was close enough to anyone to offer them a drink. Finally, she reached Rose.

"Champagne, miss?" she said, bending down.

"Yes, thank you," Rose replied. She winked at Aggie.

Aggie straightened and turned to face the young men who were talking to Rose. Directly in front of her, frozen in mid-laugh, stood Bobby Chandler. Somehow Aggie managed to keep her grip on the tray, but everything around them faded into the distance.

There was no doubt in Aggie's mind that Bobby knew exactly who she was. The laughter on his face shaded to surprise, then just before the anger, there was a flash of hurt and disbelief.

"Excuse me," he said, not to Aggie, but to the young men around him. He turned on his heel and walked away. Rose, who had seen Bobby's face from where she sat, stood up. Together, the girls watched Bobby leave the party. Neither of them moved as his tires squealed out in the quiet street.

Lightning flashed and thunder cracked almost overhead. The clouds burst and torrents of rain came down on the party. Young women shrieked, throwing flimsy summer shawls over their heads as they ran for the house. The dry earth gave off a dusty scent as the rain soaked in, like a sigh. Aggie and Rose stood, unmoving. Rain fell into the champagne flutes and bounced off the silver tray Aggie still held in her hands.

One by one, the beautiful Japanese lanterns went out with a hiss, and were ruined by the rain.

Chapter Nine

Stuart Donaldson

Aggie woke the next morning, feeling as if she had been hit on the head with a large, blunt object. She remembered going through the motions after Bobby left the party — changing her rain-drenched uniform, serving what was left of the food, cleaning the kitchen. She remembered lying in her bed awake, all night it seemed, listening to the rain. If only I can get through today, she thought.

"My goodness, Agnes, you look pale," Mrs. Stockwood said after breakfast. "Are you feeling ill?"

"I've a headache, ma'am," Aggie replied. At least the headache had its use.

"I'll help tidy the garden after breakfast," Rodney said, "since you're not feeling well. Don't worry, Mother," he waved aside her small protest. "Thanks to Agnes, I'm all packed and ready to go. In any case, the train doesn't leave until five."

He stood on the ladder a short time later, passing wet ropes and sodden bits of paper down to Aggie — all that remained of the beautiful Japanese lanterns.

"You didn't know, did you?" he asked.

Aggie shook her head.

"Did you?"

"Me! Of course not. I would have done anything to stop Rose if I had. I tried to speak with you after I saw him. Remember? When you came into the garden with the tray. I wanted to prepare you, or warn you to stay inside, or...something." He stepped off the ladder. "Last night I was worried that Bobby might talk to my father about this, but I don't think he will. He'd be too humiliated. Rose will have to deal with him now. I don't envy her one bit, but I must say she brought this upon herself...and you."

"I think I understand why she did it," Aggie said. "She thought it would be like one of those romance novels. Bobby would look at me and realize we were meant to be together. Poor Rose. I suppose I always knew Bobby never would have had anything to do with me if he'd known what I was. But that was a bitter lesson, coming face to face with him — one I'll no forget. And after the mischief we got up to, perhaps I deserved it."

"No." The voice came from behind them. Aggie and Rodney turned, and there was Rose. She was pale, but her chin was lifted defiantly. "No," she said again. "You didn't deserve to be hurt and humiliated." She came and stood beside them. "Agnes, I'm so stupid. I should have listened to you, Rodney."

"You certainly should have," Rodney said. Aggie had never heard him speak so sternly to Rose. Tears sprang to Rose's eyes, and he softened a little. "It isn't right to play with people's feelings, Rose," he said more gently.

"Oh, Agnes, I was so sure about Bobby. Now I've gone and hurt you both. Bobby's angry as anything, but I'll make him understand. Can you forgive me?" Her lower lip quivered.

Aggie sighed. Rose hadn't meant to hurt her. There was no point in being angry now. "How could I not forgive you, Rose? You've been so kind." She leaned forward and quickly hugged Rose. But there was something final in that hug. Rodney was leaving and things would never be the same.

A few hours later, Aggie stood by the streetcar stop. Her head hurt slightly less now. She looked down at her old, black shoes. They were just about worn out, but they'd have to do. But I do wish, Aggie thought as the streetcar rumbled up, that I'd not agreed to spend the afternoon with Emma and Stuart.

Over the summer, while Aggie was busy with Rodney and Rose, Emma had finally met a young man to suit her. His name was Stuart Donaldson. He was a Canadian, a gardener who came to work at Emma's employers' house every week. From what Emma had told Aggie, Stuart was the most perfect man in Canada, at the very least. The few times Aggie had seen Emma over the summer, she'd scarcely spoken of anything else. Emma had wanted Aggie to meet Stuart but somehow the day had always been postponed. Until now. When they'd planned it, Aggie had hoped it would take her mind off Rodney's departure.

They had arranged to meet near the Merrymakers Stage at Sunnyside amusement park. Too near the Palais Royale for Aggie's comfort, but that couldn't be helped now.

"Well, well, Emma, you've been holding out on me," Stuart said when they were introduced, looking Aggie up and down. "Your little sister is quite a looker." He nodded at her with an approval Aggie had not asked for and did not want. A looker! Rodney would never use a word like that — neither would Bobby.

As they walked along the boardwalk Aggie studied Stuart. His hair was parted in the middle and his face was bisected by a pencil-thin moustache. He was small and thin but he looked strong. Wiry, Aggie decided, was the word that best described him. Everything about him looked hard.

During the endless discussion of Rodney's wardrobe over the past few weeks Aggie had learned something about men's clothes. Now, she couldn't help comparing Stuart's loud, cheap jacket to the elegant clothes she had packed in Rodney's suitcases.

But Emma clearly thought Stuart was wonderful. And so, apparently, did Stuart himself. "Yes sir," he said, "It may be all right for you girls, all this please and thank you ma'am, but a man wants to be his own boss. A few more years and I'll set up my own gardening business. Pretty soon, I'll be the boss." To Aggie, he sounded as if he thought this was the best idea anyone ever had.

Aggie listened without saying much, watching Stuart and Emma together as they walked past the children's wading pool. He had a way of touching Em, just her arm or hand, that seemed to proclaim ownership. Somehow with Stuart, Emma's usual self-possessed spirit shrivelled. She spoke and acted like some spineless idiot Aggie hardly recognized.

The grass was still too wet to sit on after last night's rain, so they found a bench and watched some boys flying kites. Aggie's head still hurt, and she found herself growing more and more annoyed with this brash young man. For Emma's sake she managed to keep her opinion to herself until they walked Aggie to the foot of the long flight of stairs that lead from Sunnyside up to the streetcar stop.

"We should do this again, Agnes," Stuart said. "Say, maybe we could make it a foursome. I know some great guys. I bet they'd fall for you in a minute."

Suddenly, Aggie could hear Bobby Chandler on the night she'd met him saying, "You don't mind if we make it a foursome, do you, Stockwood?" Stuart Donaldson expected her to go out with one of his friends? Aggie said nothing, but her face must have betrayed what she was thinking because Stuart shifted his eyes away. "Maybe that wasn't such a good idea," he said. The look Emma gave Aggie held more surprise and hurt than anger.

Aggie was glad to leave them. The staircase to King Street was long and steep, but she ran all the way up. When the streetcar came, she swung herself into her seat and sat frowning at the window. Later, she got off the Yonge streetcar long before St. Clair. She needed time to think.

Why did Stuart bother her so much? It wasn't just her headache. Stuart Donaldson, she thought, is common. The idea made her angry at herself. Yes, she thought, you may want someone with fine manners and fine clothes, someone like Bobby Chandler, but someone like Bobby will no have you. She sighed. Mrs. Bradley was right; nothing good could come of trying to be someone she wasn't. And nothing had. Stuart Donaldson's friends would never suit her now.

It was almost dark when Aggie reached the Stockwood house. Rodney was gone. She could tell as soon as she came into the house—all the liveliness was drained from the place, just as surely as if it had been packed in his suitcase and taken away.

Chapter Ten

The Other Toronto

The Stockwood house was quiet again, but in the weeks after Rodney's departure, Aggie discovered that she was at least part of the household now. Mrs. Bradley and the Stockwoods had accepted her completely and the ache of homesickness that had coloured everything last winter was much easier to bear. Still, Rodney and Rose were the only real friends she'd made, and once again Aggie was alone. Emma offered more Sunday outings with Stuart, but these invitations were half-hearted. Aggie was glad that Emma accepted her refusals so readily.

But being alone was different now. Over the summer, Aggie had come to feel at home in Toronto without even noticing. She especially liked Toronto Island, in spite of the afternoon she'd spent there with Bobby, or perhaps because of it. And, with summer gone, the island was peaceful. In September and early October, Aggie often spent her half days alone on Centre Island. Sometimes she would sit in the autumn sunshine writing letters home. Sometimes she just walked across the empty picnic grounds, kicking the fallen yellow leaves. She was so lost in the beauty of these afternoons that she never noticed the tall, black-haired young man who sometimes watched her, but never tried to approach.

When it grew too cold to visit the island, Aggie began to explore the city. She quickly realized there were parts of Toronto she knew nothing about — parts that didn't seem to exist for people like Rodney and Rose. One day, just as the first snow was falling, Aggie found herself on a streetcar travelling down Spadina Avenue. Solid stone mansions gave way to a jumble of small shops that spilled their wares out onto the street in wild confusion. Many shops had signs in heavy black letters that looked nothing like the alphabet; yet Aggie recognized them from somewhere. Finally she realized that single letters in this script were printed above some of the psalms in her Bible. Aggie remembered Mr. Sheff, the tailor who loaned her mother money. This neighbourhood must be Jewish. On an impulse, Aggie got off at the next stop. Stepping from the streetcar, she almost felt as she if she was getting off the ship from Scotland again.

Aggie found herself in a market full of small shops. People spoke to one another in a language she didn't understand. It was strange, but not frightening. Everyone was busy, lively, interested in what they were doing.

A shopkeeper spoke to Aggie as she passed, pointing to his wares.

"You need umbrella, miss? Fine umbrella for rain? Just twenty-five cents."

When Aggie smiled and shook her head, the man shrugged and smiled back.

A sudden crash made Aggie turn around. A truck had skidded on the new snow, veering onto the curb and into some crates of live chickens outside a small poultry shop. Some of the crates tipped and broke open. Chickens flew in all directions. A tiny old woman from the poultry shop hurled herself at the truck driver, shouting. The truck driver, who seemed at least twice her size, stared down at the small, furious woman as if he didn't quite believe this was happening. Meanwhile, the chickens made a break for the open. One ran straight towards Aggie on nimble, yellow legs.

Aggie had never been interested in her father's pigeons, but she knew something about birds. Everyone in her family did. Now she deftly grabbed the chicken and tucked it firmly under her arm. The bird seemed to sense it was in the hands of someone who knew what she was doing. It jerked its head about and blinked, but did not struggle. By now, a large crowd of bystanders had collected. A few cheered when Aggie caught the chicken. Feeling more than a little silly, she made her way through the crowd to the poultry shop.

While the old shopkeeper continued her tirade, another woman had taken over, setting the wooden crates upright, putting things back into order. A policeman arrived. The angry shopkeeper went to him, and so did the truck driver, who still had not spoken a word.

The other woman turned to Aggie and gave her and the chicken a careful, appraising glance.

"You must be farm-girl," she said, "to catch chicken so fast, and honest too. Most of those chickens Mindl will never see again." She glanced towards the little shopkeeper, who was finally growing calmer in the shadow of the policeman.

"No, not a farm-girl," Aggie said, "but my father keeps pigeons."

The woman opened an undamaged crate and helped Aggie settle the flapping chicken inside.

"In Canada, your father keeps these pigeons?"

Aggie shook her head.

"In Scotland."

She helped the woman stack the crate with some others. Aggie had assumed that this woman must work at the poultry shop, or at some other shop nearby, but when the chickens were settled, she picked up a shopping basket.

"Why you come to Canada, honest pigeon girl?" she asked.

Her English was actually better than that — Aggie could see she was joking. She was about sixty, her grey hair covered by a scarf. Her English was a bit rough, but her pale blue eyes were full of humour. Aggie found herself explaining why she had come to Canada.

The woman gave her another steady look.

"English is the language you have always spoken, yes?" she asked.

"Yes," Aggie said, "Scots, but English."

"Good enough. My name is Hannah," the woman said. "I am servant, like you. Housekeeper for a family. They live not far." She waved over towards Spadina, the direction Aggie had come from. "This family are needing young woman to teach English. No one will come. No young woman from university, not from teacher's college either. I think maybe they are afraid of Jews." She looked at Aggie sharply. "Are you afraid of Jews?"

"No. Of course not." Aggie said, surprised by the idea.

The woman named Hannah laughed.

"I believe you. The wife of the man I work for is needing help. He will pay you well to speak English with her. You will come with me to meet them?"

Aggie considered. She could wander around alone as she had for weeks on her half days, or she could follow Hannah on what sounded like an adventure. She wasn't sure she could teach anyone. But she knew that her refusal could be taken to mean that she, too, was unwilling to help these people because they were Jewish.

"Yes, I will come," she said. Aggie had never done anything like this before. But she was sure she would be safe with Hannah.

Aggie felt a little shiver of excitement as she followed Hannah out of the market. The neighbourhood on the other side of Spadina was certainly not Deer Park. The crowded houses had tiny front yards, but most of them looked well cared for. Soon they came to Beverley Street and Hannah turned to a large brick house with a sloping roof and a big front porch, a better looking house than most they'd passed. She took Aggie to the side entrance.

Inside the spotless kitchen, Hannah waved Aggie into a chair.

"Sit. I will telephone my employer. His business is not far from here. Five minutes and he can be home." She left the room.

Aggie looked around. The icebox was not as modern as the electric refrigerator in the Stockwood kitchen. Still, these people were probably well-to-do. Aggie realized that she couldn't measure this place against the Stockwood household. The Stockwoods were simply rich.

Hannah returned as abruptly as she had left.

"Five minutes," she said. "You like tea?" Aggie nodded. "Good. I make tea." She set a tall glass in a little metal holder before Aggie, then busied herself at the stove. "I work for Moshe Mendorfsky," she said. "Moshe is a good boy. Since he was little I am looking after this house. My husband worked for Moshe's father many years. After my Jacob dies, I come here to keep house. Now, Moshe's parents also are dead. Mendorfsky's is furrier. You see ads in paper?" she asked. Aggie shook her head.

"Ads are in paper. This is quality shop, making finest fur coats in Toronto. This is inside shop. No piecework stitched by starving women and children. Craftsmen work there. They belong to union, take home good wages."

Hannah spoke with such intensity that Aggie didn't know how to reply, so she waited quietly for her tea. Hannah poured it into the glass when it was ready. There was no milk in sight. Aggie heard the front door open, then she heard voices at the front of the house. A few minutes later, a man came into the kitchen. Aggie began to stand, but he indicated that she should stay seated. From the grey beginning in his hair, Aggie guessed he was about forty. He was tall and thin with clear brown eyes.

"Here is Agnes Maxwell, English maid," Hannah said. "Agnes, here is Reb Moshe Mendorfsky."

"Hannah, I won't even try to guess how you found this young woman," Moshe said. His voice was gentle, and he spoke clear Canadian English with only a trace of an accent. He turned to Aggie. "Would you excuse us for a moment, please?"

"Yes sir," Aggie said.

They went into the hall outside the kitchen. From where she sat, Aggie could hear a quiet, heated conversation in a language she did not understand. She only knew that Mr. Mendorfsky was asking questions, and Hannah seemed to be insisting on something. After a few minutes, they returned to the kitchen.

"Hannah says you are a domestic?"

"Yes sir, I work in a house in Deer Park."

"Deer Park. Some of our customers live there. You have how many half days off?"

"Just two sir. Today and Sunday afternoon."

Moshe nodded.

"My wife Rachel came from Russia less than a year ago. She speaks little English. I have looked for a young woman to help her, a native English speaker. I imagine Hannah told you how difficult we've found that." He gave a wry smile.

"Sir," Aggie said, "I'm not sure I'd be the best person to teach English..."

Moshe waved her protest aside.

"Hannah feels it will be good for Rachel to have someone to talk to, and I must agree. Do what you can to help with her English. I will pay you five dollars a month to come here on your half days, to make conversation with Rachel. Is this agreeable to you?"

Five dollars was a great deal of money. Aggie could not refuse.

"You do not mind working on your half days?" Moshe asked.

"My family is still in Scotland, sir. All my extra money goes home until they can come to Canada."

Moshe smiled.

"Many Jews do the same thing. I can see we will get along. Could you start now, today?"

"Well...yes, I suppose I could."

"Excellent. Now you will meet Rachel."

Moshe led her to the front parlour. They passed a small room whose walls were completely lined with books. In the parlour, Aggie was startled to find a beautiful, sad-eyed girl who looked no older than Aggie herself.

"This," said Moshe, "is my wife Rachel."

Chapter Eleven

Rachel

Rachel Mendorfsky sat by the window. When she saw Aggie with her husband she put her sewing aside and smiled, but the smile did not erase the sadness Aggie saw in her eyes, nor the dark circles under them. She was beautiful in spite of that, with her dark curls and delicate features.

Slowly, clearly, as if speaking to a small child, Moshe spoke to her in English.

"Rachel, this is Agnes Maxwell. She will come to speak English with you every Thursday and Sunday afternoon."

Rachel nodded.

"I am pleased to meet you," she said shyly in heavily accented English. To Aggie it sounded as if she had memorized these words.

"I must go now," Moshe said. He quickly kissed his wife on the forehead and was gone. An uncomfortable silence followed. Aggie didn't know what to do. She looked through the books stacked on a small writing desk near her and found an atlas. She took the book and sat near Rachel, and they began to look at maps of Europe and North America. Rachel pointed to a part of Russia near Poland.

"My home," she said.

Aggie pointed to Russia, then Canada.

"How did you travel to Canada?" she asked.

Rachel traced a route on the map.

"Poland," she said, "Germany, then boat." She drew her finger across the Atlantic. "Bad," she said softly.

"You do not like Canada?" Aggie asked, trying to speak as simply as possible.

"Not Canada," Rachel said. "Russia. Is very bad." For just a moment, she looked frightened, then she shook her head. Aggie picked up another book quickly to change the subject. When the clock on the mantel struck five, Aggie could hardly believe the time had passed so quickly. She hadn't imagined that talking to Rachel would be work, but she returned to the kitchen exhausted.

"So," Hannah greeted her, "how is English teacher?"

"I dinna think I'll make much of a teacher, Hannah," Aggie said.

"You will be good for Rachel, I am sure."

"Mrs. Mendorfsky seems very shy."

"Only Mrs. Mendorfsky in this house was Moshe's mother. You call Rachel 'Rachel.' You need supper on your half days?"

Aggie nodded.

"You eat here," Hannah said.

Aggie started to protest, but Hannah refused to listen.

"In this house is plenty of food. You are too thin. You eat my good cooking, get nice and fat," she said.

Aggie laughed.

"Won't Mr. Mendorfsky mind?" she asked.

"In this kitchen, I make rules," Hannah said. When she put a bowl of hot chicken soup on the table, Aggie suddenly realized how hungry she was.

"Rachel is near your own age, no?" Hannah asked as Aggie ate.

"Yes, she is."

"And you wonder how she came to be here." This was a statement, not a question.

"Yes," Aggie said, grateful that Hannah was willing to satisfy her curiosity.

"Rachel comes from same *shtetl*, same village in Russia where Reb Isaac was born, Moshe's father," she said. "So her father is *landsman*." She used the Yiddish word. "This is very important to Jews. We find help for our *landslayt*, the people of our homes. Many years after Reb Isaac comes to Canada, Rachel's father marries younger woman. They have only Rachel, then his wife dies. He is old man when Rachel is born. When Rachel's father is dying, his wish is to have his daughter safely out of Russia. Russia is bad for the Jews. People in the *shtetl* know Reb Isaac Mendorfsky is now rich man in Canada. When they come to Toronto, he helps them find work. Three years ago, when Rachel's father is sick, he writes to Reb Isaac. But Reb Isaac is dead. So the letter comes to Moshe. They write back and forth, and Moshe agrees to bring Rachel here, to marry her."

Hannah saw the look of surprise in Aggie's eyes.

"This is how it is done in old countries, Agnes. My husband was found for me by matchmaker. This is the old way. Here is not the same. Now the young ones find husbands and wives without matchmaker. But Moshe never thinks of wife, only his business and reading books. Many mothers put their daughters in his way —nice girls. He never sees them. I think, this one will never marry. But then, the letters come from Russia. The idea of saving Rachel from so hard a life makes him happy." Then she chuckled. "Also, he sees photograph. Rachel is beautiful. If she is ugly then the idea might not seem so good."

She left the stove and sat at the table with Aggie.

"Now is very difficult to bring young woman from Russia, different from when I was young. Canada now wants only the English, the Scottish, and from a few other countries. The Jews are good people for Canada. But Canada has closed its door to the Jews. So Rachel must come to Canada as sponsored domestic servant."

"Just like me!" Aggie said.

Hannah smiled.

"Not like you. We must apply to government, promise to employ her. This is only way she can enter Canada. A few months later, Moshe marries her." Hannah sighed. "But now Rachel is not learning English. Only old women like me speak Yiddish. To make friends with young wives, Rachel needs English."

"But would one of those women not teach Rachel?"

Hannah hesitated for a moment before replying.

"I think yes, if Moshe asks, but he is proud." Then Hannah dropped her voice. "At first, many women are happy to visit Rachel, but they find her shy, and...as if she is not there. To visitors she seems unfriendly. So they come less often, now not at all. Too many days I find her crying. And Rachel never goes out."

"Never?"

Hannah shook her head.

"This morning, I say to myself, Rachel is too much alone. This day, I will find someone for her. I see you with chicken, I think, this girl has kind face. Moshe is not so sure, but I know I am right. You will be a friend to Rachel." This sounded like an order rather than a prediction.

Later, Aggie rode home on the streetcar feeling as if she had travelled much farther than a few miles that day. She knew she would have to tell the Stockwoods she was working on her half days. As her employers, they had a right to know. But she had no idea how they might react. Mrs. Bradley was sitting in the kitchen when Aggie came back.

"Have you eaten?" she asked.

Aggie nodded. It was hard to believe this was the same woman who had once given her a piece of dry toast for breakfast.

"Tea's on the stove," Mrs. Bradley said, "a fresh pot."

Aggie poured herself a cup and sat at the table.

"I had a letter from Rodney today," Mrs. Bradley said. Rodney wrote both his mother and Mrs. Bradley every week without fail. Usually, Aggie was interested in Rodney's letters. Tonight, she only nodded. "You're somewhere else this evening," Mrs. Bradley said.

Aggie nodded again.

"I've taken a job on my half days," she said and she explained everything, starting with the chicken in the market.

"And these people are Jews?" Mrs. Bradley said when Aggie finished. She frowned. "I'm not sure what the Stockwoods will say. They feel responsible for you, Agnes. You'd better ask."

So Aggie spoke with Mr. and Mrs. Stockwood the next evening when her work was finished, repeating the whole story.

"Agnes, this is most unusual," Mrs. Stockwood said. "These people are not Christian. I'm not sure it's proper for you to be exposed to them. What would your parents say?"

"I think my parents would approve, Mrs. Stockwood," Aggie said, and she told them about Mr. Sheff in Scotland.

Mrs. Stockwood seemed flustered when she finished.

"Borrowing money from these people is one thing," she said. "Working for them is quite another." Too late, Aggie realized that the idea of borrowing money was probably embarrassing to someone like Mrs. Stockwood.

"What did you say the name was?" Mr. Stockwood asked.

"Mendorfsky, sir,"

"And he's a furrier? Well, I'll make inquiries — see if I can find out anything about these people. Then Mrs. Stockwood and I will make a decision."

If Aggie had any doubts about wanting to help Rachel, they vanished over the next few days. She knew the Stockwoods were only doing what they thought was right. She also knew that she would have to abide by their decision, unless she wanted to work elsewhere. But she was sorry they felt it necessary to interfere.

By Wednesday, Mr. and Mrs. Stockwood had still said nothing.

"Do you think they've forgotten?" Aggie asked Mrs. Bradley at lunchtime.

"I couldn't say," Mrs. Bradley said.

"But Mrs. Bradley, tomorrow is my half day!" Aggie couldn't keep the exasperation from her voice.

"Well, if they haven't said anything to you by this evening, I'll ask."

But that evening, as she finished the dishes, Aggie was called into the sitting room. Her hands trembled a little as she dried them on her apron. She wasn't entirely sure she would be able to hide her anger if the Stockwoods said no. If only Rodney was here, she thought. He'd make them understand.

Mr. Stockwood lowered his paper to his lap.

"Well," he said, "It seems half the men I know have bought fur coats for their wives at Mendorfsky's." He smiled. "Everyone speaks highly of this young man. He runs a good business and his coats are excellent."

"I hope you remember that at Christmas, dear," Mrs. Stockwood said.

Mr. Stockwood smiled.

"Since we know something about these people, Mrs. Stockwood and I have decided that you may take on this extra work. Be careful, though," he added, "that you don't teach this young woman to speak with a Scottish accent." And he laughed.

Aggie felt herself relax.

"Aye, sir," she said, smiling, "I mean, yes sir."

Aggie went back into the kitchen feeling as if she had won a prize. Now Emma was her only concern. Giving up her half days meant that she would almost never see her sister. Even if she didn't like Stuart, Aggie still wanted to see Emma sometimes. She put the problem to Mrs. Bradley.

"Well, these folks are willing to give you your supper, but maybe you could meet Emma for supper once in a while, or even just a cup of tea before you come back here."

"Oh, Mrs. Bradley, that's exactly what I'll do."

When she met Emma on Thursday evening, Aggie was excited and pleased. But Emma greeted the whole idea with at least as much suspicion as the Stockwoods had. Aggie tried to explain to Em why she was happy to help Rachel, but Emma remained unconvinced.

"I'll never understand you, or Mum either." Emma said. "Mum with her tea for the tinkers, her kind words for that old Mr. Sheff."

"But Emma, but for Mr. Sheff neither you nor I would be here today."

Emma snorted.

"Aye, and he gets wealthy off the likes of us."

Aggie considered. If Mr. Sheff was wealthy, why would he work so hard? But she wasn't willing to argue with Emma.

"Better you than me," Emma concluded when she saw that Aggie had nothing more to say. "You'd no find me making friends with heathens."

Chapter Twelve

A Tea Party

All winter, Aggie travelled between Deer Park and Beverley Street on her half days. Rachel seemed to look forward to her visits. They found it difficult to talk at first, but Moshe helped Rachel practice her English between visits and soon the two girls conversed more easily. Mrs. Stockwood even gave Aggie some old children's picture books that had once belonged to Rodney to help with Rachel's vocabulary.

When Rachel saw them, she said, "That is a good youdea."

"Youdea, Rachel?" Aggie said, perplexed.

"Yes," Rachel replied, impatient at Aggie's apparent slowness. "Youdea. I have idea, you have youdea." Aggie could not help but laugh, and when she had explained it, Rachel laughed too. It was the first time Aggie heard her laugh. Then Rachel said, "Please excuse my missing understanding." Aggie didn't have the heart to correct her again.

Another day, as they sat looking at the atlas together, Aggie said, "Maybe you could write letters in English, Rachel. It would be fun for you. But we'd need some addresses."

It was Rachel's turn to look puzzled.

"Why we need summer dresses to write letters?" she asked.

It took Aggie a minute to understand.

"Oh...not summer dresses, some addresses."

"This is what you say. Summer dresses."

Aggie finally wrote both phrases out before Rachel understood. Then they began to giggle.

"We could write some addresses on summer dresses," Aggie said, and they laughed even harder. When the commotion brought Hannah from the kitchen, the two girls couldn't speak for laughing. Finally, they managed to explain, and that set them off again. Tears of laughter streamed down Rachel's cheeks. For the rest of the visit, whenever their eyes met, they both burst into giggles.

At the end of the visit, when Aggie ate in the kitchen, Rachel joined her for the first time. They were still sitting together when Moshe came home. He looked a bit surprised to find Rachel in the kitchen. But she greeted him with a kiss and a smile that quickly chased any hint of disapproval from his face.

One afternoon, watching Rachel bend over a book in the late winter sunlight, Aggie realized that she loved this girl in a way that she had only ever loved her younger brothers and sisters. She wanted to make Rachel happy.

But Rachel's laughter did not always come readily. There were still days when she was slow to even smile. One Sunday afternoon, it was clear that Rachel had been crying. Aggie said nothing, but near the end of the visit Moshe came into the room. He was carrying two tickets which he laid on the table for Aggie to see.

"Horowitz, the great pianist, is coming to Massey Hall," he said. "Do you know of him?"

Aggie shook her head and Moshe continued.

"Like Rachel, he is an emigré from Russia. I was sure she would like to hear him play. His concerts are always sold out. These tickets were very hard to find. And she refuses." Aggie could see he was struggling to keep his temper. Rachel sat with her head down, miserable. Obviously, the discussion of these tickets had been going on for some time.

"Agnes," Moshe continued, "Rachel cannot spend the rest of her life inside this house. She has been happier since you started coming here. She is fond of you. Please, talk to her." The despair in Moshe's eyes went straight to Aggie's heart.

"I'll do my best."

Moshe nodded and left the room. The tickets remained on the table.

Rachel's head stayed down, and after a moment, Aggie saw a tear fall into her lap. Reaching into her own handbag, Aggie took a clean handkerchief and pressed it into Rachel's hands.

"Rachel," she said softly, "can you no talk about this? Why you must always stay inside?"

Rachel wiped her eyes and looked at Aggie. When she spoke, her voice was barely a whisper.

"You know this word *pogrom*?" she asked. Aggie shook her head. "In Russia," Rachel said, "many times are pogrom." She hesitated and sighed. "Men come to burn houses, to kill animals, also...to kill Jews — this is pogrom. After my father is dead, while I am waiting to come to Canada, there is pogrom in my village. Men come with guns, set fires. I see from where I hide in the attic. Some young men try to stop this, I know them all my life...and these people murder them."

Aggie's breath caught sharply in her throat.

"But the police," she said, "did they no stop this? Did they punish the murderers?"

Rachel smiled sadly.

"Police are always somewhere else when pogrom happens. Unless they lead. In days of Tzar, they tell us, this is wrong but we cannot stop. This is lie. They know, they *encourage* pogrom." In spite of her agitation, Rachel said this last sentence proudly. "Encourage" was a new word for her. "When communist revolution happens, many Jews are happy. We are told now pogrom will stop. But this is also lie. Nothing changes, and still there is no punishment for those who murder Jews."

Both girls sat quietly for a moment. Aggie wondered what she could possibly say in the face of such injustice. She reached out and took Rachel's hand.

"Rachel," she said, "I don't understand why bad people are not punished, how there can be such hate in the world." Aggie paused. "But now you are in a different country, you have a different life. If you let what has happened ruin your life, it will be as if...as if the pogrom continues in your heart forever."

Rachel nodded.

"It does," she said. "The ones who die, I live my whole life with them. Now they are dead. On that day, part of me dies too."

Aggie remembered her brother Dougie. It wasn't the same, she knew, but in another way it was. She thought about a story her mother told her after Dougie died, when Aggie had not been able to stop mourning.

"Rachel," Aggie said, "I'm going to tell you a story. Once, in Scotland, where I was born, a long time ago, there was a mother who had a wee bairn — a child, only one child. She loved him very much. But her child grew sick and, although the mother did everything that could be done, he died. Nothing could comfort that mother. She felt as if the child had died through some fault of her own. She tore her clothes and wouldn'a comb her hair. And every day, for a year, she did nothing but greet — I mean cry. She hoped that death would come and take her too, but somehow she lived, and she blamed herself even for that.

"After a year, the angels took pity on her. They decided to let her see her child in heaven. So she dreamed of a beautiful, happy place where all the children were running barefoot and free —except one little child who was weighted down by a big glass jar, full to the brim with water. The child carried this burden everywhere, and this was the woman's own son. When the woman saw this, she said, 'Why is my child punished?' And the angel said, 'The water is your tears. As long as you mourn your child, he must carry the weight of them.'"

Aggie paused.

"My mother told me that story after my brother died. I always loved my brother. He was so full of life. I thought my heart had broken into a million wee pieces, and I would never feel anything but sadness again. Is that how you feel?"

Rachel nodded.

Aggie smiled a little.

"I didn'a like my mother very much for telling me that story. By then, my sadness was almost like a friend. But I knew she was right. Dougie would not have wanted me to ruin my life. And those young men who died in your village would not have wanted that from you." Aggie stopped speaking now. She was appalled to realize that she was crying too. Surely this couldn't help Rachel.

Rachel spoke quietly.

"Agnes, you are good friend to tell me story from your mother. Now, I need to think. You go to Hannah. I will see you next day."

Aggie left the parlour. She felt miserable. Moshe had asked for her help, but it seemed she'd only upset Rachel more. Perhaps she'd even made things worse. She was also shocked by what Rachel had told her, and deeply ashamed. Rachel had been too kind to say so, but the people who carried out those pogroms probably called themselves Christians. Hannah looked dismayed when Aggie came into the kitchen.

"Little Agnes, something is wrong?"

"Everything," Aggie said. "I told Rachel a story to make her feel better, but I think I only upset her more. Hannah, I dinna think I can eat my supper today."

Aggie left the Mendorfsky household as quickly as she could. She had to walk all the way to Bloor Street before she felt calm enough to board a streetcar.

Over the next few days, Aggie worried about Rachel constantly. On Thursday, she sat nervously on the streetcar wondering how she would be received.

Hannah opened the back door and let Aggie in to a kitchen filled with the smell of fresh baking. Two beautiful honey cakes were cooling on top of the stove.

"Rachel is upstairs," Hannah said. "You wait a few minutes."

"Did Rachel go to the concert at Massey Hall?" Aggie asked.

Hannah shook her head.

"She tells Moshe she is not ready." Then Hannah smiled. "But she comes with us today to the market."

"She's coming outside? Oh Hannah, that's wonderful."

"She says she will go out if you are with her. Moshe says that is fine, but he asks me to come too. I know Toronto much longer than you or Rachel."

Then Rachel appeared, wearing a new winter coat. It was wool, a lovely shade of plum, with deep fur trim at the collar and cuffs. It was cut according to the very height of fashion, falling straight to the knee without any trace of fullness. Her hair was completely hidden under a small cloche hat in a lighter shade of lilac, and she wore leather gloves. Aggie still wore the old coat she had brought from Scotland. She only realized how hungrily she must have been looking at Rachel's outfit when Rachel spoke.

"You like coat? Moshe has it made for me. The collar and cuffs, he makes pattern himself. The fur is silver fox." Rachel smiled nervously.

"It's beautiful," Aggie said.

When the front door opened a few minutes later, Aggie wasn't entirely sure that Rachel would cross the threshold. She hesitated for a long moment, then finally stepped outside.

"You show me where you meet Hannah," she said. But when they reach Spadina, Rachel was taken aback by the width of the street and the traffic. She turned pale and whispered, "We go home now, please. Next time we go to market."

Aggie and Hannah exchanged a quick, worried look, then turned back towards the Mendorfsky home. But it was a start.

On Aggie's next visit, when they reached Spadina, Hannah grasped Rachel firmly by the elbow and guided her across the street before she could react. In the market, when Rachel saw the little shops she said, "Here is like my home," and her eyes shone. Her cheeks grew rosy in the winter air.

Aggie could see that the shopkeepers didn't quite know what to make of this wealthy-looking young woman in her chic clothes at first. But when Rachel heard Yiddish, she began to speak excitedly in her own language. Neither Hannah nor Aggie had the heart to make Rachel use her stiff English and the pretence of a lesson was forgotten. Rachel chatted and laughed. After that, Rachel went out with Hannah and Aggie often, and then with Moshe. She lost her pale, haunted look.

One Thursday, Aggie returned from the Mendorfskys to find Rodney sitting at the kitchen table with Mrs. Bradley. Except for the parcels she'd already mailed home, Aggie had almost forgotten about Christmas. When Rodney rose and took her hand, Aggie recalled the distant day last spring when he had kissed that hand and she had wondered if she ought to be afraid of him.

"Well, Agnes," he said, "I understand you've been busy. Tell me all about it."

And Aggie did. Mrs. Bradley had never asked Aggie about the Mendorfskys and Aggie assumed she was not interested. But now, when she told Rodney about Rachel and the pogrom, Mrs. Bradley's eyes grew bright with tears.

"Poor little mite," she said. "How could anyone be so cruel?"

"That's what I wondered as well," Aggie said.

"I have friends at university who wouldn't believe what you've just told me, Agnes," Rodney said. Aggie started to protest, but he held up his hand. "Oh, I don't doubt that you've heard the truth. Not for a minute. It's just that people only believe what they want to. It's good, though, that you're helping this girl."

"Well, really, if you think about it, the Mendorfskys are helping me."

"Yes, that's true, but I'm happy to see you've found something serious to do. You always did impress me as a serious person. Well, more serious than Rose at least."

"I suppose we'll be seeing Miss Rose again," Mrs. Bradley said, "now that you're home."

"Well, actually no," Rodney said. "Rose's father finally let her tour Europe with her aunt, the one who lives in Buffalo. They're spending Christmas in Rome."

"Well now, how ever did that happen?" Mrs. Bradley asked.

"From what Rose told me in her letters, it seems that Bobby intervened on her behalf."

Aggie felt herself grow red at the mention of Bobby's name. Rodney noticed, but pretended not to.

"Yes," he continued, "Bobby decided that Rose ought to have more to do with her life. To keep her out of mischief, she said in her letter."

Later that day, Aggie met Rodney in the second floor hall.

"Is Rose happy, do you think?" she asked.

"I believe so. It was good of Bobby. He could have been quite spiteful after what happened. He's a better person than I thought." Rodney hesitated, then went on. "Agnes, there's something else I think you ought to know." Rodney took a deep breath. "Bobby Chandler is engaged to be married. The wedding is planned for this summer. I wouldn't have told you," he rushed on, "except I thought you might hear from my mother or Mrs. B."

"I understand," Aggie said. It was thoughtful of Rodney really. "Is he marrying someone you know?" Aggie knew she shouldn't ask but she couldn't stop herself.

"Well, no. Rose said she's a secretary in Bobby's office."

"Oh," Aggie said. She felt as if she'd been punched in the stomach. Maybe Rose didn't know the difference between a secretary and a domestic, but Bobby obviously did. "Well," Aggie said, "I must go — there's ironing to do."

"Yes, of course," Rodney said. He seemed relieved that the conversation was over.

As she ironed one of Mrs. Stockwood's dresses, Aggie thought about Bobby Chandler. She had barely known him. Why, then, should she suddenly want to go to her room, shut the door and cry? It wasn'a love, she told herself, only the hope of love. Was that enough to cry for? Maybe it was.

When Christmas came, Aggie found it hard to believe that the holiday involved such elaborate preparations. In Scotland, Christmas was a quiet religious holiday. All the lively celebrations were saved for hogmanay, at New Year. Now the Stockwood house filled with the scent of pine and the spicy smells of Mrs. Bradley's baking. The Christmas tree fascinated Aggie. She had never seen one before. It was hard to believe anyone would put a live tree in the sitting room.

Rodney still had a few weeks at home after the celebrations were over. But Aggie noticed that he was not as relaxed as he might have been. Then, one day when Aggie came down for lunch, she found Mrs. Bradley and Mrs. Stockwood in the kitchen together looking glum.

"Well, I suppose we knew it had to happen someday," Mrs. Stockwood was saying. "We'll survive." Then she turned to Aggie. "I'm afraid we won't be seeing much of Rodney this summer."

"Is anything wrong?" Aggie asked.

"No, not wrong exactly. Really, I suppose we should be pleased. Rodney has been offered a research position with one of his history professors next summer. It's quite an honour really. It just means that he'll be staying in Kingston and we'll only see him from time to time. He knew we'd be disappointed. That's why he waited until after the holidays to break the news."

When Rodney went back to Kingston, Aggie returned to her usual routine. Soon it was February. It was hard to believe she had been away from home for almost a year. On her birthday, Mr. and Mrs. Stockwood called her into the sitting room after supper.

"Well, Agnes, you're eighteen today," Mr. Stockwood said. "We know how much you want to bring your family to Canada, so we thought we'd give you a small raise. From now on, your pay is thirty dollars a month."

"Thank you very much, sir," Aggie said. She smiled broadly. In her mind, she was already calculating what that money would mean to her family.

"Yes, well...we wanted you to know that we appreciate all the hard work you do for us," Mr. Stockwood said.

"What he means to say, dear," Mrs. Stockwood said, "is that we'd be lost without you now."

"Thank you, ma'am," Aggie said. As she slipped from the sitting room into the kitchen, she felt like cheering out loud. Her mother's next letter said that perhaps they would be able to bring the family to Canada before the end of this new year.

After the holidays, Rachel occupied most of Aggie's thoughts once again. Before Aggie knew it, the piles of snow on the sidewalks had dwindled, and the buds on the trees were beginning to swell. One early spring day Aggie brought the photograph of her younger brothers and sisters to Rachel.

"Look, Rachel," she said, "these are my brothers and sisters."

"Yes?" Rachel said, taking the photo from her hand with interest. Aggie pointed them out by name, and told Rachel something about each. Then she told Rachel the story of the money in the church collection basket and how it had ended up in Jen's lap.

"It was a special collection too," she added, "for the heathens in China."

"What is heathen, please?" asked Rachel.

"Heathen means godless," Aggie said.

"Then you and I are not heathens," said Rachel firmly.

"No," Aggie replied, "we certainly are not."

"Are these all your brothers and sisters?" Rachel asked.

"No, I have one sister, Emma, who is here in Toronto like me." She did not mention Dougie again.

Rachel's eyes widened when she learned of Emma.

"Yes? You have a sister in Toronto?" The idea excited her. "I will meet her," she said.

"Oh, Rachel, I'm not sure that would be proper." Aggie wondered if Emma could even be persuaded to come.

"No matter," Rachel said. "You are my friend. I will speak to Moshe."

Moshe could not refuse his Rachel. Now it fell to Aggie to talk to Emma, who was both flattered and appalled by the idea.

"She wants me to come to tea?" she asked in disbelief. "What a strange lot you've fallen in with, Aggie."

Still, Aggie could see the idea appealed to her. The Mendorfskys were wealthy enough to interest Emma.

"You could wear your new green dress, Em, the one Stuart gave you." Aggie coaxed. "And Rachel will treat you just like a guest."

But the mention of Rachel reminded Em.

"Aggie, I dinna think I can. They aren't like us — you say so yourself."

After, Aggie realized she should have taken Emma's feelings to heart, should have let her say no. But she was so caught up in the idea of making Rachel happy that she coaxed Emma into accepting.

One bright afternoon in April, Miss Emma Maxwell was received at home by Mrs. Rachel Mendorfsky. Rachel planned the event like a state occasion, consulting with Aggie on the menu for tea the week before, choosing and discarding half a dozen perfectly nice dresses until she settled on just the right one.

On the day of the tea, Aggie was filled with uneasiness. Emma was probably not what Rachel expected. But when Aggie arrived, the Mendorfsky house was filled with the welcoming scent of Hannah's freshly-baked honey cake. At two o'clock sharp the doorbell rang and Emma sailed through the front door dressed in her finest.

"Welcome to our home," said Rachel, smiling, when she was introduced.

"Yes, thank you," said Emma, but there was no feeling in her voice. Instead of looking at Rachel she gazed around as if she were in a museum.

"Emma, we'll be taking tea in the parlour." Aggie said, taking her by the arm to get her attention. "In here," and she steered her sister out of the hall.

Rachel, Aggie and Emma sat stiffly in the parlour. There didn't seem to be anything to say. Aggie was relieved when Hannah arrived a moment later with a tray of cake and an English teapot. She studied Emma while Rachel poured the tea.

"This one looks nothing like you, Agnes," she said at last.

Emma looked at her as if a stone had spoken but made no reply. When Hannah left, she turned to Aggie and said, "Who says sisters have to look alike, eh Aggie? Silly old woman," she added under her breath. Aggie was annoyed but could say nothing.

The conversation lurched uncomfortably along after that, starting and stopping. Aggie managed to get Emma to talk for several minutes about Stuart, but then silence fell until Emma, who never could abide silence, decided to take the lead.

"Well," she began, "Aggie tells me that you came to Canada as a domestic just as we did. I must say you've done quite well for yourself." Aggie choked on her tea.

As Emma and Rachel patted her on the back, Aggie longed for the moment when she could walk her sister to the streetcar. But the afternoon dragged on. Hannah's honey cake was the only thing that seemed to please Emma.

Finally, the party was almost finished, Aggie hoped.

"Will you have more tea, Emma?" Rachel inquired.

"No, thank you, but I will have a wee bit more of that heathen cake," said Emma. Heathen cake. Aggie could not believe she had heard those words.

Rachel said nothing, but blushed deeply as she lifted the cake on to Emma's plate with a silver knife.

Somehow, Aggie managed to drink the rest of her tea and make more meaningless conversation until at last it was time for Emma to leave. Never in her life could Aggie recall being so angry with her sister. She let Emma walk to the streetcar by herself, afraid of what she might say if they were alone. She never wanted to see her again. When the door closed, Aggie turned to face Rachel.

"I thought my friend's sister would be like my friend," Rachel said simply.

"Oh, Rachel," was all Aggie could say.

Chapter Thirteen

Like the Swallow

The next Sunday, when Aggie came to visit Rachel, Moshe asked to speak to her alone.

"Agnes," he began, "I must thank you for helping Rachel to...to overcome her troubles from the past. And her English is much better. I think she began to learn so quickly so that she could speak with you. But, you know that Rachel has suffered greatly in the past from the...intolerance of others. I must protect her from ever being hurt in that way again."

"Sir, I'm so sorry..." Aggie began, but Moshe silenced her.

"Please. This isn't easy for me. I have decided it would be better for Rachel to begin to spend her time with women who are...more similar. You understand, don't you?"

Aggie nodded miserably. She did understand. But she had to ask one thing.

"Does Rachel want this as well?"

"Rachel was terribly hurt, I'm afraid. I think she understands that I want what is best for her." He handed Aggie an envelope. "Here is the money for this month, and something more. We wish you every happiness in life."

Of course, Aggie had realized that she couldn't go on visiting Rachel forever. But she had hoped that they would remain friends. Emma had changed that. Aggie pushed the envelope unopened into her purse, mumbled something polite and left. She almost fled the house, but she could not go without saying goodbye to Hannah. Aggie had every intention of remaining calm and strong, but Hannah obviously knew what had happened and the pity in her eyes melted Aggie's resolve to nothing. Hot tears welled up before she could stop them. Hannah took her own hanky to Aggie's face, as if she was a small child. After she dried Aggie's tears they sat down to talk.

"Moshe wants only to keep his Rachel from hurt, Agnes. She has been hurt too much in life. You understand?"

Aggie nodded.

"Rachel is not happy with this," Hannah told her. "We talk about it."

"Then why..." Aggie's voice trailed off. She could hardly put the question into words.

"To fight, to argue, this is not Rachel's way. Moshe looks at Rachel and he sees girl who would not leave this house. Girl who needs always to be protected. Rachel will show him she has changed. Then you will be welcome here again. But this takes time. Maybe weeks, maybe months. Rachel will not forget you, Agnes. When she makes Moshe understand, she will let you know."

Aggie left the Mendorfsky house feeling somewhat better. But what hurt most of all, she reflected on the streetcar going home, was that Rachel had not said goodbye. It wasn't until later that night at bedtime that Aggie thought to open the envelope. Inside, along with a ten dollar bill, Aggie found a note:

My Dear Friend,

Moshe says that my time for speaking English with you is over. But I will always remember your friendship. I hope you will not forget me. May your family come to Canada soon. Someday, you come to tell me so.

And it was signed, 'Rachel.' Aggie felt the tightness in her heart relax a little. Hannah was right. Some day she might be able to go back. For now, that hope would have to be enough.

Still, there was Emma to contend with. Aggie had to admit that what happened with Rachel was partly her own fault. She had ignored Emma's misgivings. If I hadn'a insisted, she thought, things would be different now. Aggie knew as well that Emma had not been deliberately rude to Hannah or Rachel. Emma was not polite by nature. In the world they came from, manners counted for very little, but to the people Aggie and Emma worked for they meant a great deal. Because Emma was not polite, she never was treated as kindly by her employers as Aggie was. But, Aggie could not help thinking now that Emma's rough ways made life hard for more than herself.

After the tea at Rachel's, Aggie avoided Emma, not trusting her temper. Finally Emma phoned.

"Would you like to meet me this Thursday after your lesson, Aggie?" she asked. Emma sounded unusually meek.

"There are no more lessons," Aggie said. Let Emma ask why, she thought.

There was pause on the other end of the line.

Then Emma said, "Well, if you're free again, maybe you'll spend this Sunday afternoon with us, pet." "Us" meant Emma and Stuart, of course. But Emma sounded contrite and Aggie realized this was intended as a peace offering. Still, she could not bring herself to say yes. An outing with Stuart was hardly a prize. As usual, Emma could not stand silence. "We'll go anywhere you want," she added.

"The island," Aggie said without a second thought. All winter she had longed to be there. Her choice was not intended to vex her sister, but it did.

"Oh, Aggie, it's too early to go to the island. It will be cold and damp, and nothing is open yet. Stuart will hate it," Emma protested.

Aggie was not inclined to make Emma's life any easier at that moment.

"It's that or nothing. Do as you please," she said. And so it was.

Next Sunday afternoon was sunny and warm, the first taste of the summer to come. Even though Aggie was still angry at Emma, her spirits rose as she travelled down to the ferry docks under a cloudless sky. But the chilly breeze off the harbour made Aggie pull her sweater around her as she approached the nearly empty ferry docks. At first, she could not see Emma or Stuart. Then she noticed them, leaning against a rail, heads together. Stuart's arm was over Emma's shoulder. Aggie felt like an intruder. Ordinarily, her natural modesty would have made her shy. But today she forced herself to interrupt them.

"Hello, Em," she said.

Emma and Stuart turned around.

"Oh hi, Agnes," Stuart said. "Nice day, eh? Emma thought we'd have a picnic."

"We bought some sandwiches and ginger ale," Emma added quickly. Aggie could see that they were both trying to be nice to her. Instead of cheering her, this only added guilt to her resentment, making her feel even worse.

Only the smaller ferries were running this time of the year. When they boarded the *Primrose* a short time later, Stuart insisted on paying Aggie's fare along with Emma's and his own. Aggie already had her own streetcar ticket ready, and had to stop herself from arguing with Stuart. As the ferry slipped from its moorings at dockside, Aggie wished that Stuart and Emma would stop making it so hard for her to enjoy being angry. Luckily, as soon as the boat was under way, Stuart and Emma folded in on themselves again, shutting Aggie out completely. They scarcely noticed when she left them to explore. Aggie remembered to look for the *John Hanlan*, the old ferry that Rodney had said was going out of service last summer. He must have been right. The *Hanlan* was nowhere in sight.

"Well," Stuart said as they stepped off the ferry, "it's pretty quiet this time of year. Good thing we brought our own grub. I'm starved. Let find a spot for this picnic."

They found a sheltered place and ate their late lunch on the grass. The sweet scent of sun-warmed grass filled Aggie's lungs. Out of the breeze, the afternoon sun felt hot on her back and again she felt the irresistible lift of spring.

As they ate, Stuart casually read the newspapers that had wrapped the ginger ale bottles. "Look at this, Em," he said. "Pretty soon they'll be starting the blossom time excursions. We could catch a boat just by the ferry docks, steam over to Port Dalhousie, and take the train to see the blossoms. There's even dancing on the boat on Saturdays."

Emma leaned on his shoulder and sighed.

"That'd be lovely Stuart, but I never have Saturdays off, and you know I'm not allowed out that late."

"I know you're hardly allowed out at all," Stuart grumbled. "Why don't you think about a factory job, Emma? Lots of places take girls. You'd earn more and you'd always have your evenings free."

Aggie waited for Emma to tell Stuart that factory work was out of the question. If Emma worked in a factory, she'd need to board somewhere. She'd spend more money on clothes. She'd need to pay for meals and laundry. The extra wages would be eaten up, and the money that Emma would be able to send home would dwindle down to nothing. Tell him! Aggie thought, but Emma just smiled.

"Oh, Stuart, I'd have to think about it," she said.

"Well, you'd better," Stuart said. It almost sounded like an order. Aggie tried to imagine what Emma would say if anyone else had spoken to her like that.

It was obvious that Emma and Stuart wanted to be alone. Aggie finished her lunch as quickly as she could and walked away from them, crossing a bridge over a lagoon. She couldn't believe that Stuart would try to persuade Emma to take a factory job. Or that Emma would even consider it. The thought gave her a hollow feeling in the pit of her stomach. Without Emma's help, it would take twice as long to bring the family to Canada. Could Emma be so selfish? she wondered. Aggie realized that she didn't know her sister well enough to tell any more. She followed the lagoon inland. This is a good place for writing letters, she thought. I wish I'd brought some paper. Oh well, at this rate I'll have all summer to come out here alone and write my letters.

Aggie sat down under a tree and dozed a little, never actually sleeping, but not really awake either. Spring cleaning was just finishing up, and she was more tired than she liked to admit. She lost track of time until finally she noticed that the shadows were getting longer. I'd better find Emma and Stuart, she thought. But that wasn't quite as simple as she'd expected. Soon she had to admit she had no clear idea where she was.

She found herself in a field edged by willows. Evening was approaching now and the light changed, making everything sharp and luminous. Across the field, blue-black swallows cut the air, diving in a perfect, wild dance. The swallows reminded Aggie of the brooch Davy had given her, and of Davy himself. She'd almost forgotten Davy, but she remembered him now. It would be so good to have him beside her to ease this ache of loneliness. Aye, she chided herself, and turn you into someone like Emma, someone who cares more about some strange man than her own family. Would it be possible, she wondered, to fall in love and keep that love from changing you? That isn'a something you need to worry about just yet, she told herself.

The willows were full of long, plain flowers. Aggie leaned her cheek against a branch to catch their woody scent and the golden pollen brushed her face. Suddenly she heard a voice, a man's voice, singing. It was so close that she startled at the sound, but she realized at once that the singer was unaware of her. His voice was low and rich and true, a voice that might sometimes sing for others, but just now it had a quiet, private sound. The sound of someone thinking to himself. He sang,

She's like the swallow that flies so high,
She's like the river that never runs dry,
She's like the sun that shines on the lee shore
She loves her love, but love is no more.

Quietly, Aggie edged around the tree. On a bench a few feet away the singer sat with his back to her. He was a tall young man with broad shoulders and neatly cut black hair.

His tweed coat had seen better days, but it was not cheap or vulgar. Beside him was a cloth cap like those the men of Loughlinter wore.

He stopped singing and seemed lost in thought. Aggie wondered what kind of face would belong to that gentle voice, but she was too shy and too fearful of strange men to make her presence known. She slipped away without being seen. When she came to the next clearing, she saw the bridge and could finally retrace her steps to the ferry dock. Emma and Stuart were waiting. The *Primrose* was approaching.

"Aggie Maxwell, where have you been?" Emma said. "We were just about to miss the ferry because of you."

It was almost a relief to hear the annoyance in Emma's voice. Aggie was tired of being treated kindly by her sister.

"I was confused," she admitted, "not really lost..."

"Oh, I get it, not really lost, you just didn't know where you were," Stuart said and Emma laughed.

The ferry pulled into the slip. The day of being nice to Aggie was over.

The sun was setting as they boarded the ferry. Just before it left the dock, Aggie saw a young man run across the grass and swing himself onto the boat at the last possible moment. He moved with a careless ease and joked with the crew of the ferry at the dunking he'd just missed. He pulled his cloth cap down over his black hair, laughing at himself. Aggie recognized the singer.

As the boat glided slowly towards the city, Aggie looked back at the island. She found the field of willows where the young man had sat. From here she felt a shock of recognition. Surely she knew this picture from somewhere. Then she realized: it was as if she had been walking in the stained glass windows at the Stockwood house. She felt like someone touched by magic. Now, she thought, I want to have a look at that young man.

Aggie never thought of herself as the kind of person to be noticed. She felt she was neither pretty enough or plain enough to attract attention, and this gave something like invisibility. So when she slipped away from Stuart and Emma a few minutes later she expected to be able to satisfy her curiosity about the singer without his noticing.

She sat on a bench not too far from where he stood, then moved her gaze over to him in what she hoped would be a casual manner, as if she hadn't noticed he was there. A shock of straight hair fell neatly across his forehead. It was so black it seemed to gather the light around it. His eyes were as blue as the sea had been on the morning Aggie sailed into Halifax harbour. His clean-shaven jaw was straight and firm. He was as handsome as that wistful, deep voice she had heard. All this she saw in a brief instant. Then their eyes locked. Aggie hoped he would ignore her. Instead, he smiled and moved away from the rail — towards her. Aggie looked away quickly.

He's going to come over, Aggie thought, her heart pounding. She almost rose to run away, but she realized she could hardly do that on a ferry. And anyway, she told herself, there's the crew here and Stuart and Em. He canna harm me.

He seated himself on the bench beside her, but not too near.

"I know you," he said to her surprise. "Last October month you walked out on the island alone. I sometimes thought to speak with you." He spoke, not in the swaggering way of most young men, but quietly and directly. His accent was something between English and Irish but Aggie couldn't place it.

"Well, you'd have frightened me to death if you had," Aggie said, half smiling.

"I thought as much. Well, maid, Will Collins'd never do you no harm." Aggie wondered how he knew she was a maid. He looked at her with something like regret. "You never noticed me? The women sometimes do." With any other man, Stuart for example, those words would have been a boast. But he made them into a gentle joke.

Aggie shook her head.

"No, not in the fall." But she didn't like the disappointment in his eyes, so she hurried on. "But I noticed you just now, on the island. You were singing a song, about swallows, I think. I heard you. I was behind the willows."

He smiled broadly at this and slapped his thigh in delight.

"You never were!" he exclaimed. "Right behind me and I didn't know? We'll have to put a bell on you, my dear." It took Aggie a moment to realize he meant like the bell on a cat, and he was joking. He paused now, looking out across the water but there was nothing uncomfortable in the silence. "I come here often myself." he said. "It's not like my home at all, but the water makes me feel at home. You know what it says in the psalm? 'He leadeth me beside the still waters, He restoreth my soul.'"

"But where is your home?" Aggie asked, "I've never heard anyone who speaks quite like you."

He grinned.

"Knew I wasn't a Canadian, did you? You're a clever maid. I'm from Newfoundland."

"Newfoundland?" Aggie said. "I remember Newfoundland. It made me feel better when I was coming to Canada." She told him about the rocky cliffs and the lights from the little villages that had made her feel less seasick and less homesick.

"You sailed right past the place I belong to," Will said. "The place where I was born, I mean. I've sailed those same waters myself right often." And he began to tell her stories of big, full sailed ships called banking schooners that plied the waters off that coast, looking for schools of fish so the men could put out in dories, little boats that came to a point at each end and could be stacked, "like mussel shells," he said, on the deck. "I was only twelve when I first took a berth on a banking schooner," he told her, "working like a son of a..." he stopped himself just in time, "...working like a man." He ended with a grin that made her laugh in spite of herself.

Aggie enjoyed Will's stories so much she scarcely noticed the boat was docking. Emma and Stuart rounded the deck to find her sitting with a stranger, laughing. Emma looked amazed. Aggie never spoke to strangers.

"Aggie," she said sharply, "come along now, we'll be going."

Aggie rose and was relieved to see that Will did too.

"I'll just come along with ye crew, if no one minds," he said.

Stuart decided to mind.

"Now wait a minute, mister," he said. "I don't recall anyone introducing you to the young lady." He was at least six inches shorter than Will and looked like a bantam cock squaring off in front of him.

Will looked down at him mildly.

"Well, my son, you weren't here, so I did the honours myself. Now, who would like to introduce her to me?" he asked.

Aggie was surprised by the sound of her own voice.

"I've been speaking for myself for quite some time now, thank you all very much. Will Collins, I'd like you to meet my sister, Emma Maxwell and her friend Stuart Donaldson, and I am Agnes Maxwell." She took his hand for a moment. It was warm and calloused and it covered hers completely. She liked the feel of it.

"Pleased to make your acquaintance," Will said formally, and he and Aggie walked off together. Aggie was pleased to see that Emma was speechless.

Aggie was somewhat astonished herself. She walked towards the streetcar loop, shadowed by the unfamiliar height of this man (for she barely reached his shoulder), wondering how this had happened. She had never done anything so reckless in her life, except perhaps when she went with Hannah — and that was different.

When they reached the streetcar loop Will said quickly, "Do you mind if I see you home?" Emma and Stuart were just about to catch up. There was no time to think.

"Yes," Aggie said, "I mean no," she added quickly. "I mean..." Stuart and Emma arrived. Aggie composed herself. "Mr. Collins has offered to see me home, Emma, so we'll walk over to the foot of Spadina and make our way from there." That would take them well out of Emma's way.

"Spadina!" Emma said. "That's not even on your way. Aggie, I hardly know you tonight. If you wish to go traipsing off with some stranger, suit yourself. But dinna blame me if they find you at the bottom of the lake." The last sentence she hurled after Aggie like a curse. Aggie stopped and went pale.

Will stopped, then took a small notebook and a pencil stub from his pocket and wrote something down. He tore the paper out and gave it to Emma.

"That's my name and address," he told her, "and the place I works to. If any harm befalls this maid tonight, you give that to the police. Now mind you puts that somewhere safe," he added with a smile. Emma took the paper without a word.

"Pleasant woman, your sister," Will commented as they walked away.

Chapter Fourteen

Will Collins

Will pointed to a boat as they walked away.

"That one there, the *Sir Francis Bond-Head*, we sailed she right up to Lake Superior. Now that's as fair a body of water as ever I hope to see. Put me in mind of my native Newfoundland, it did, the coastline right wild and rock bound, as you yourself remember," he smiled down at Aggie.

The idea that he was a sailor made Aggie's heart sink.

"So I imagine you spend a good deal of your time away?" she asked.

"No, maid," Will said, "I sail no more. Thought I'd try my luck ashore about a year ago. I had my reasons..." he began, then suddenly fell silent.

Night was coming on now, and this part of the city was full of factories and warehouses, deserted on a Sunday evening. But when Aggie looked up at Will she felt she had nothing to fear.

"I've flattened your ear long enough, my dear," he said. "Tell me something of yourself."

"Well, you know I come from Scotland, and you know my sister Emma." Aggie couldn't help but smile, recalling the look on Emma's face when she took Will's slip of paper. "And you know I'm a domestic servant..." she continued.

"I do? You told me no such thing," Will said.

"Aye, that's true, but you called me a maid."

Will laughed and Aggie felt a little hurt. This must have shown, because he stopped at once.

"Maid is just a word we use where I comes from," he explained. "It means a young girl. What do you say in Scotland?"

"We say lass or lassie, and a young boy is a lad."

"We say lad too, or youngster, but a girl is a maid. I didn't know you were a domestic at all, my dear."

"And do you call everyone my dear?" Aggie asked, teasing.

"My dear and worse, my dear," he said laughing. "My duckie, me darling, me young trout..." he began to list. "That's just our way where I belong."

"Well, Aggie is what they call me at home."

"Then I will call you Aggie, and perhaps you'll call me Will."

They walked along in the brisk night breeze, the pungent smell of the lake in the air. When she drew her arms around her and shivered a little, Will took off his jacket and gently placed it on her shoulders without touching her. It smelled pleasantly of pipe smoke and sweat. Aggie found Will easy to talk to. She told him of her family in Scotland, and her work in the Stockwood house. She told him about Rodney and the wristwatch last spring, but not about Bobby Chandler. When they reached the foot of Spadina where they might have boarded a streetcar, Will said, "Perhaps, if you're not beat out, we might walk a ways more."

"That would be fine," Aggie said. Her legs were beginning to ache, but she wanted this evening to last.

"You're not hungry are you?" Will asked. "We could stop in to a cafe somewheres around here."

Even though she'd eaten nothing since the picnic lunch, Aggie shook her head. She was far too excited to eat. As they walked up Spadina through the Jewish neighbourhood, Aggie thought of Rachel. Without meaning to, she told Will about Rachel and how Emma had upset things.

"Well, I can see how Emma might," Will said. "She has a tongue like a gaff hook, that one. But it seems to me that these people were unfair, telling you not to come back because of something your sister did."

Aggie considered this seriously before replying. She noticed Will kept silent, letting her think.

"I dinna think so," she said at last. "They paid me well, even gave me my supper if I wanted. The Mendorfskys were kind to me. Rachel's husband felt he had to protect her from being hurt."

"But you were hurt in this as well, my dear," Will said. "Who protected you?"

"No one," Aggie replied. "Since I came to Canada, I've learned to take care of myself."

Aggie was surprised at the pride in her voice. Maybe Will would think she was boasting.

He looked down at her and smiled, but it wasn't a teasing smile.

"I can see that," he replied. He was perfectly serious. Aggie liked him for that.

"Well," she said after a moment, "you've told me your stories, but not about yourself. Tell me about your family."

For the first time, Will seemed uncomfortable. He hesitated, then spoke reluctantly.

"I've no family to speak of, just myself. There only ever was my mother. I was eleven when she died. From then on, I fended for myself. I fished and sailed. I came to Canada three years ago. About a year back I left the boats. Now I work on the high steel, building those skyscrapers you sees from the lee shore of the islands. You've seen the Royal York Hotel?" he asked.

"Yes, of course."

"Well, I worked on she for more than a year. She's almost finished now. My job was over a few months ago."

"Oh," Aggie said. "That was the first thing I saw the day I came to Toronto."

Will smiled.

"Well, there's a good chance I was up there. I'm working on something smaller now, just an addition to a factory. But I've got my eye on that new Bank of Commerce building. It's no more than a hole in the ground now, but they'll be needing me soon. Thirty-two storeys, she's going to be. Tallest building in the British Empire."

"It sounds as if you like your work," Aggie said.

"I do. But still, I sometimes miss the water."

"Why did you leave the boats then?"

Again Will seemed uncomfortable.

"There were reasons," he said, and then he smiled. "It's a long story. Perhaps I'll tell you when I knows you better. In any case, when I'm working up high I can look out to the lake and see the ships passing sometimes. They likes us New-foundlanders on the skyscrapers because we're right fearless on the heights. Spent our lives scrabbling up and down the rigging of vessels till all the fear was drove out of us, see? That's not boasting," he added quickly.

Aggie laughed.

"I didn'a think it was. But my feet are tired now," she said, hating to admit it. "And there's still a long way to go. Could we catch a streetcar at the next stop, do you think?"

Will nodded.

"Whatever you like, Aggie my maid."

When they finally stood before the Stockwood house it didn't seem possible to Aggie that the long journey from the ferry docks had flown by so quickly. She shyly removed Will's jacket from her shoulders and held it out to him.

"This is where I live, Will. Thank you for seeing me home," she said. She wanted to see him again, but she had no idea how to let him know. There was an awkward pause, then Will began to talk so rapidly that Aggie almost had trouble understanding him.

"When I said I saw you last October month, I used to watch you from afar, walking, writing...and I'd think to myself, I wish I could know that maid. But somehow I knew if I came after you I'd only drive you off. And then, I thought, perhaps there's some fellow she's writing to, perhaps she's spoken for. I could hardly believe my luck when I saw you aboard the ferry tonight. I'm an honest man, Aggie Maxwell, and sober. Would you walk with me if I calls for you?"

Aggie was so overwhelmed she could only nod.

Will looked a little disappointed.

"Well then, will I see you again?" he asked.

"Thursday is my half day," Aggie said. She knew it wasn't much of an answer. Her words came out in a whisper.

"My shift is finished at four," Will said, "I'll need time to wash up after. Would you meet me for supper at five?"

Aggie didn't trust her voice, so she nodded. Will took out his small notebook and pencil again and wrote down directions.

"Do you think you can find this place? I often eat there. It's on King Street West."

"Yes," Aggie said. She couldn't think of another word to say.

Will looked at the ground. She could see things were not going as well as he would have liked.

"Well then," he said, "goodnight to you, maid. I'll see you on Thursday..." he hesitated, "...if you do want to meet me again, that is." And he hurried away without even a handshake.

If you let him go off like that, Aggie told herself, you may never see him again. She finally found her voice.

"Will," she called after him.

He turned around.

"Yes, my maid."

"I will. Want to see you again, I mean."

Will's grin almost gave off a light of its own.

"Well, I'm some pleased to hear that, my dear. I though you were only trying to be polite."

Aggie shook her head.

"I'll never say anything just to be polite to you, Will Collins."

"I'll hold you to that, my maid," he said, and he was gone.

After the chill spring night, the Stockwood kitchen seemed flooded with warmth and yellow light. Although she had only left it a few hours before, Aggie saw everything as if for the first time: the bright blue dishes stacked neatly on the drain board, the stove that Mrs. Bradley kept blindingly clean, the faint and pleasant after smell of food. Nothing had ever seemed as beautiful or vivid. As she made her way upstairs in a daze she wondered if love might do this to someone.

Or maybe she was getting sick.

When Aggie woke up the next morning, she knew she was not sick. It was as if the mere fact that Will existed on this earth had taken away all the pain she'd felt since she left her family. But before she even left her bed, she made herself a promise. No matter what I feel for Will, I'll not make a fool of myself. I'll no be like Emma is with Stuart.

Although Aggie had promised herself not to act silly, her happiness could not be hidden. She flew through her chores, humming to herself until finally Mrs. Bradley said, "You've met some young man, haven't you?"

Aggie blushed and nodded.

"How did you know?"

"Well, you'd never guess it now, but I was young once myself. Actually, I'm surprised it's taken this long. A pretty girl like you, I expected the boys to be flocking around way before now. I thought to myself, she must be mighty particular, that Agnes of ours."

Thinking of Bobby Chandler, Aggie blushed again.

When the mail came at noon Aggie had a letter from home. Letters did not come often enough, but Aggie knew that was because her mother had so little time. Eagerly, Aggie ran up to her room and tore this one open. She read:

My Dear Aggie,

I hope this letter finds you well. The children and your Da send their love. We've counted our pennies and it seems we will be able to come to Canada in August or September. We never could have done this without your help, my brave lass.

I must tell you another thing, and I do not know how you will take the news. I was to see the Canadian Doctor when he was in Loughlinter, to speak with him about having the children's needles. He knew as soon as he saw me that you would soon have another little brother or sister, sometime in July he says. I thought honestly that my time for such things had passed and I laughed at him, but now I know he was right. I hope you and Emma pray for us, and look forward to meeting your new wee brother or sister when we come to Canada.

And it was signed, as always, "love, Mum." Aggie was amazed that her mother would tell her such a thing. Until now, births were never discussed. Emma would be kept home from school, or later from work, the midwife sent for, and the new baby simply seemed to arrive. Aggie was happy, but somehow the news seemed unreal, perhaps because it was happening so far away.

Later that afternoon, Emma telephoned. This was rare. The telephone was still a luxury in most houses and servants were not encouraged to use it. Aggie expected Emma to say, "Well, I see you're not at the bottom of the lake." But, to her surprise, Emma sounded worried, even contrite.

"I'm sorry we fought yesterday, pet," she began. "Did you have a letter from Mum?"

"Aye, Emma..." Aggie began, but Emma continued without stopping.

"Aggie, could I see you on your half day, do you think? We'll have tea, just the two of us. I need to talk to you."

Aggie wondered if this was really Emma. She was about to agree, but then remembered Will.

"Not this half day," she said quickly. "I've...I've made plans." Aggie wasn't about to let an afternoon with Emma ruin her dinner with Will.

There was a pause on the other end of the line.

"Aggie, could you no..." Emma started, then she seemed to change her mind. "Sunday then. Will you meet me Sunday?" And Aggie agreed.

The week passed with painful slowness. The hands on the clock dragged no matter how hard Aggie worked. Finally, Thursday afternoon came. Aggie put on her prettiest weekday dress, a violet cotton print freshly washed and ironed. It was beginning to fade now, but there would be no money for new dresses this summer. Maybe after her family was settled in Canada. Then she washed her face and brushed her hair. She decided to leave it loose, just pinning it back from her fine, sharp features. She was about to leave her room when she remembered something. Going over to her bedside table, she opened the small velvet box Davy had given her, took out the swallow-shaped, marcasite brooch, and pinned it on.

Aggie spent the afternoon in Simpson's, shopping for a birthday present for Jen. This was the second birthday of Jen's that Aggie had missed. It was hard to believe she would be eight before Aggie saw her again. Aggie made the shopping last as long as she could, and still it was only four o'clock. Somehow, time seemed to have stopped altogether. She forced herself to browse among dresses she couldn't possibly afford and today was not even particularly interested in, until! at last it seemed reasonable to head down to King Street West.

Aggie found the cafe ten minutes early. Rather than stand on the street, she went inside. Will was already waiting at a table for her. He stood when she came in and pulled out her chair. He was wearing a spotless white shirt and looked so pink and clean that he might have been washed with a scrub brush. He didn't bother to hide his pleasure.

"I'm some happy to see you, Aggie maid," he said. "I thought perhaps you'd change your mind."

Aggie shook her head, suddenly shy. Will seemed to understand her shyness. He steered away from personal questions while they ate, telling her stories about the seal hunt instead.

"I travelled to St. John's just the once, to get a berth on a sealing vessel. The seals comes up on to the pack ice in the spring to pup, see? The ocean turns right white — a sea of ice. Sometimes, on a foggy day, the light seems to come more from the ice than the sky, almost as if the world were upside down. And everything right silent, still and calm...but the ice bears in on the ship till all the timbers creak. You wants a wooden vessel on the ice, because it gives. I seen square hatches in the deck of that vessel pushed to diamonds by the pressure of the ice."

Aggie listened spellbound until finally the meal was finished.

"But here I've been going on the whole time, never giving you a sliver of silence to slip a word into, my maid," Will said. "You've been shopping I see," he nodded to Aggie's parcel on the table.

"Aye, my wee sister's having her birthday in June. My Mum and Da haven't money for presents, so I try to make sure there's something," Aggie said.

"Tell me more about your family," Will said, and Aggie did. Will seemed hungry for details, asking her all the children's names.

"I've a photograph of them," Aggie told him.

He seemed pleased.

"Next time, you bring it and show me," he said.

Next time. Aggie liked those words.

"We hope they'll be in Canada by the end of the summer. There's going to be a new baby too." She told him about her mother's letter.

"Still a lively couple then, your parents," he said.

Aggie looked at him curiously.

"What do you mean?"

"Oh, nothing," he said quickly. "Listen, maybe this Sunday you'd come with me to me brother's?" he asked. "A crowd from home gets together some nights, and I said I'd bring you along."

"I promised to meet Emma on Sunday afternoon, but I'll be happy to meet you later. But Will...I thought you said you had no family."

He'd blushed then for the first time.

"Well, he's like me half brother, see? We share the same father. But tell me, where do you think your family will live when they comes here? Will you be looking for a place?"

It wasn't until much later, alone in her room that night, that Aggie realized how quickly Will had changed the subject, how embarrassed he'd looked. It's almost as if he's hiding something, she thought.

Still, he seemed to be someone she could trust. More than that. When he shook her hand that night outside the Stockwood house, she had wanted to press her face against the clean white cotton of his shirt and feel the warmth of him under the cloth, to smell the scent of his skin. Aggie had never felt anything like this before. Not with Davy, not with Bobby Chandler. Sitting on her bed now, brushing her hair, Aggie wondered why.

She'd been fond of Davy and she'd admired Bobby. But this was different. This was more. It was as if Will had opened a door to a place in her heart that she never knew existed, a place filled with new emotions. Aggie, who had always feared the touch of men, realized that she was not afraid of Will. She was amazed.

At the same time, a small shiver ran down her back — a different kind of fear. They had just met, but Will was already this important to her. In some ways he was still a stranger. How could she feel so much for someone who might decide not to see her again? It was enough to make her panic. I have to stop, she thought, before I feel too much, before I'm hurt too badly. But then she thought of Will, who he was, and how happy he made her. The panic subsided. It's too late, she thought. I have to trust him.

On Sunday the weather turned colder and by afternoon the sky was dark. It began to rain just as Aggie left the house, and she doubled back to borrow an umbrella from Mrs. Bradley. Emma had arranged to meet in a park, but by the time Aggie arrived, it was pouring. Emma looked pinched and nervous.

"Can we go somewhere dry, do you think?" Aggie asked.

Emma nodded.

"There's a wee tea shop just around the corner. I could use a cup. Aggie, pet," she said when they settled themselves at a table, "thank you for coming."

"What's wrong, Em?" Aggie asked.

Emma seemed to change the subject.

"You had a letter from Mum this week?"

"Aye, I did. We'll have to think about finding them a place to live, Emma," Aggie replied, remembering what Will had said.

"And what did you think of Mum's news?" Emma asked, frowning.

"About the baby? Well, I'm pleased, of course."

"Och, Aggie, you're such a child. It's almost indecent at their age. That sort of thing."

Aggie looked at her sister blankly.

"What sort of thing?"

Emma glanced around.

"I suppose you have to know some day, and it might as well be from me. Forget tea," she said shortly. "Let's go to the park where we can talk."

"The park?" Aggie cried, looking out at the hard rain. "Emma, are you daft?" But Emma left without looking back. Aggie could only follow.

They walked in the park, cold and wet under their umbrellas, for some time before Emma spoke.

"Aggie, where did you suppose babies came from all this time?" she finally asked.

"Well..." Aggie paused. It was painfully difficult to speak about these things, even with Emma.

"Did you no wonder?"

"I knew there must be things I didn'a know," Aggie confessed. "I suppose I was happier not knowing."

"Well, you're old enough now that you should know," Emma said. "A man and woman have to...to lie together to make a child. That's what makes the man the father." Emma went on to explain. There was no tenderness in her account, only the raw physical facts. It sounded to Aggie like a brutal act, something a woman would only subject herself to if she wanted a baby very badly. It seemed impossible to believe that any woman she knew had ever willingly participated in such a thing, let alone her own mother.

"But Em, how do you know this? Did Mum tell you?" she finally thought to ask.

"Oh, Aggie, dinna be daft," Emma said. "Can you imagine Mum talking about this?"

Aggie had to admit she couldn't.

"Then how...?"

Emma lowered her voice.

"Stuart told me," she said. "Stuart wants...he says he'll leave me if I won't."

Aggie was horrified.

"And he's no offered to marry you?"

Emma stared at her feet and shook her head. When she spoke her voice was scarcely audible.

"No, he hasn'a. But I dinna want to lose him, Aggie. What will I do?"

"Emma," Aggie said, "Stuart has no right to force himself on you. What would become of you if he left you with a baby?"

Emma said nothing.

"My feet are fair soaking," Aggie said finally. "Please Em, let's have some tea."

They went back to the cafe where they dried out a little and warmed their chilled bodies. Emma was quiet, dry-eyed, and calm. It seemed to Aggie as if her sister had already gone somewhere she was not prepared to follow. Aggie was relieved to let the subject go, but she had to ask one question.

"Emma, you know I don't care for Stuart. I wonder what you see in him."

"It's not hard to guess, is it?" Emma replied. "You never seem to mind working so hard, being so poor. But I do. Stuart Donaldson is going to make something of himself, Aggie. With a man like that, I might never have to worry about money again."

"What are you going to do, Em?"

Emma rested her chin on her hands. She was silent for a moment, then she said, "I canna say."

Aggie didn't know whether Emma meant that she did not know, or she would not tell, but Aggie knew she couldn't probe any further.

It had stopped raining when Aggie said goodbye to Emma. For the first time all afternoon, Aggie thought of Will. This morning, she had planned to tell Emma about Will. But she hadn't said a word about him. Now, she realized with a shock, she was glad. Suddenly, her feelings for Will were all muddled up with what Emma had just told her. The streetcar rumbled up and Aggie boarded it. Imagine, she thought, every person I see here is a product of that act. She felt ashamed, embarrassed. Then she remembered what Will had said about her parents still being a "lively couple." He knew! He knew and he'd even joked about it. Maybe he was no better than Stuart.

When she got off the streetcar a few stops later, Will was waiting for her. His eager smile faded a little when he saw her face. They walked a few blocks in near silence, Will's attempts to make conversation dying quickly one by one, until finally he turned to her and said, "Aggie maid, what's troubling you?"

She couldn't talk at first, but she knew she needed to. Besides, underneath her anger, she had known as soon as she saw Will again that he was not Stuart Donaldson and never would be. So, little by little, the story of her meeting with Emma came out.

"He said he'd leave her if she wouldn'a...do that with him," Aggie ended. Her voice dropped to a whisper.

Will laughed and reached out to pat Aggie's shoulder, but she misunderstood.

"You!" she cried. "Dinna touch me. You knew about this all along and there you were, laughing at me. Making a joke of my own mother and father."

Will looked as if he'd been slapped. When he spoke, his voice was low and gentle.

"Of course I knew. Reared up where I was, who would let me forget?" He sighed. "I had hoped to know you better before you heard this from me, but I see it's time. Forget my brother's for tonight." They passed a small park. "We'd better sit down," Will said. "There's a story you must hear."

The bench was just dry after the rain. Will sat, studying his hands in his lap, not looking at Aggie at all.

"My mother was a school teacher," he began. "Only eighteen when she came to the harbour and met my father. He was the son of the merchant in the place I belong to. Handsome as the devil, they always said of him, and well accustomed to getting what he wanted. It wasn't long before he wanted my mother. She trusted him. That was her sin — she trusted the wrong man. She believed that he would marry her. But she was wrong. When she told him that...that I was to be born, he dropped her like a live coal. Her own parents wouldn't have her back to her home then. She couldn't teach, she had no money. She had to bring a bastardy case against that man, to sue him for our keep."

Will stood and began to pace as he spoke. Aggie sat transfixed by his story.

"I grew up in that place, and there was not a living soul but knew how I was begot on my mother. 'Bastard,' they called me, every one, sometime or other." He stopped pacing. Aggie could feel Will's anger and shame radiating like heat across the space between them.

"Slapped me down with it, they did, every time I tried to hold my head up. While that bastard who was my father lived in comfort and not a one would say a word against him. He married another maid while I was still at my mother's breast. Three children they had, two girls and a boy. How I hated that young boy, George. Born on the right side of the sheets, a little prince.

"My mother always told me it was wrong to hate." He sat down again and looked at Aggie. The anger drained from his voice.

"Well, she was right. She died when I was eleven, and I began to work like a man, as you knows. About a year ago, I learned young George is in Toronto. I wanted nothing to do with him. But it's a small circle, the crowd from home, and we got to know each other. He can't stand the old man, wants no part of the family fortune. We gets along now. I feel as if I've found a brother. All those years we were youngsters, we might have been friends."

He paused and looked down at this hands again.

"Now you knows. I was afraid to tell you, you being so proper a maid, I thought you'd be ashamed of one such as me. A bastard. And it may be that you'll not want to see me again. But Aggie, maid, I swear on my own mother's grave, I will never leave a woman or a child as that man left us. When I father a child on a woman, I'll stay with them both till I die."

Aggie felt so many things at once, she didn't know what to say. She was quiet for so long that Will finally stood again and turned away from her.

"I'll see you home if you'll allow me to," he said. "If not, I understand."

She could hardly speak for fear that she might cry.

"No," she said at last. "I won't let you see me home, Will Collins." She rose and stood in front of him. "It's far too early."

A slow smile spread over his face as the meaning of her words took effect. She reached up, standing on tiptoe, and kissed him quickly. He put his arm around her shoulder and they left the small park together.

Chapter Fifteen

The John Hanlan

Will took Aggie to meet George next Sunday night. On the streetcar on the way over, he told her about the rooming house.

"Lived there myself at one time when I first arrived," Will told her. "We all gets together Sunday evenings to make a bit of music, have some fun. I'm sure you never heard the like of it before. Up half the night we are, and off to work bleary-eyed Monday morning."

Then he told Aggie about his half brother.

"He's eighteen now, three years younger than myself. He wants a bit of looking after, young George does. You see, he's never had to fend for himself, and worse, he's always had the old man telling him what to think and do. He had a rough time of it here at first, and some of that from me."

Will smiled ruefully as he spoke.

"But after I got to know him, I left off sailing and came to live nearby. We works together, on the same sites and I keeps an eye on him. You see, Aggie, I spent my life looking after myself alone. Truth of it is I'm glad to have someone else to look out for."

So that was why Will had given up sailing and settled in Toronto. Aggie was touched by Will's kindness to this boy he might easily have gone on hating, and grateful to George for inadvertently bringing Will to her.

The big rooming house off Parliament Street was run by a stout old woman named Mrs. Byrne and was filled to the rafters, it seemed to Aggie, with young men from Newfoundland.

"Pleased to meet you, my dear," she greeted Aggie. "There's been no end of talk from George about meeting Will's young woman. You're always welcome here, maid. Let me show you my house." And she steered Aggie away from Will before she could reply. The house had seen better days, but it was fairly clean.

"We're some glad to see Will take up with a young woman," Mrs. Byrne said as they toured the house. "Lived with us when first he came here, between ships, that is. Never saw a young man like him, and I've seem more'an my share in this place. So sad he was then, and haunted-like. I suppose he left home to get away from his past, but it was plain to see it was all bottled up inside of him. When he first learned young George was moved here too, he was right savage. They fought and argued — once or twice I thought they'd come to blows. Mind you," she added, "George is the kind to get himself into scrapes. But Will finally made his peace with George. And it changed Will a lot. Put some ghosts to rest I'd say, and I'm some glad. Now, come along and meet the whole crew."

When Aggie returned to Will, he had only a moment to introduce her to George before an eager chorus of voices called him to give them a song. So he left Aggie standing shyly with his brother. George looked nothing like Will at all. He was small, even delicate looking, with curly blond hair.

To Aggie it seemed that George was still a boy, whereas Will was a man. Aggie and George listened while Will sang about a ship that was lost with all hands while loved ones slept unawares at home. Then, when someone took up the accordion and Will played the spoons to keep time, George spoke to Aggie.

"If Will's the first Newfoundlander you've met, you'll be thinking we're all right clever with music and stories, but that's not so. Will is something special." Aggie did not need to be told her Will was special, but she liked the boy's easy admiration of his older brother.

"Will told you something of our circumstances, didn't he?" George asked, less easy now. Aggie nodded. "Our father's a miserable man. He makes life difficult for everyone around him. Will's life was hard at home, no doubt of that, but he was better off living out of the old man's shadow. I came to Toronto to be me own man. I wasn't expecting to know Will, much less for him to take a liking to me. And he didn't at first. But I finally made him understand that I'm not my father's son any more than he is. Now we got that out of the way, we gets along fine."

Then the accordion was put aside and Will was asked for another song. He sang "She's Like the Swallow," the song Aggie heard him sing the night they met. Listening, she realized it was not a song about swallows at all. Will sang of a young woman picking roses to give her love. When she went to him, her lover said:

How foolish, foolish you must be,
To think I loves no one but thee.
The world's not made for one alone,
I takes delight in everyone.

Then the young woman lay down and died. As Will sang, the rowdy crowd grew silent and respectful, his true, low voice filling the room. It was as if he had carried them home to Newfoundland. When the song ended, everyone was perfectly still for a moment, remembering quiet harbours and dark forests far away. Will himself broke the silence.

"Come now, Edgar," he said to the accordion player. "Give us another."

As the music filled the room, George said to Aggie, "That's Will's own song, you know. Made it for his mother, after she died. After my father heard it, he drove Will out of the place—made sure no one would give him a place to live. That's when he first went to sea." Then Will came over and took Aggie's hand.

It was late before anyone would let Will leave. Finally, Aggie sat on the empty streetcar, her head resting on Will's shoulder.

"How do you like me brother, then?" he asked her.

"He's no like you, is he? But I like him."

"And what do you like best about him?" Will persisted. It occurred to Aggie that she had spent most of the evening with George. She raised her head from Will's shoulder and looked at him.

"What do I like best about George? Oh, he's a bonny lad and I like him for many things." The disappointment in Will's eyes made her sorry for teasing him even this briefly, so she hurried on. "But best of all, I like the way he loves his brother, as well he might. We have that in common, George and I."

Will looked as if he wasn't really sure what he had heard.

"You wouldn't just be teasing me now, would you, Aggie maid?" He tried to say the words lightly, but Aggie could see how serious he was.

So she grew serious herself.

"No, I am not. I love you, Will Collins."

He was silent for a long moment, then he put his hand over hers.

"Not since my mother died has anyone said those words to me, Aggie. And I love you as well."

After that night, Aggie and Will were together as often as they could be. George sometimes came with Will on Aggie's half day. Aggie and Will would have preferred to spend their time walking together on Centre Island, or anywhere quiet, but George liked excitement. After Sunnyside opened again in May, they usually went there.

One night in June, they walked around the rides and games of chance, eating redhots. Sometimes, Aggie caught glimpses of the lake across the road, calm on this gentle night. I wish, she thought, that Will and I could sit down there. But she knew that wouldn't suit George.

The carnival attractions were in full swing now. This week, a large tank was set up, topped by a high diving tower.

"Look at this," George exclaimed, reading the sign beside the tank. "The flaming Helkvists, sensational European fire-divers, will plunge from a 90-foot tower, with bodies aflame, into a flaming tank."

Aggie shuddered. "That's something I'd rather not see."

"You're some timid, Aggie maid," George said. "Well, let's try our luck at the ring toss, Will. Perhaps we can win a teddy bear for Aggie."

"And what do I need a teddy bear for, George?" Aggie asked. "I'm no a child."

Will reached into his pocket and handed George a quarter.

"You go ahead, my son. Perhaps Jen would like one," he said. Will had learned so much about Aggie's family, it seemed as if he knew them. Aggie smiled up at him.

"I'm sure she would."

"George got himself in trouble at work again today," Will said as soon as his brother left, "pranking with hot rivets. I'm not sure how much longer he'll last. Born to trouble as the sparks fly upward, he is." Will had found work for both of them on the new Bank of Commerce building, the one he'd told Aggie about the night they met.

"Well, maybe we'd better keep an eye on him now," Aggie said. George was just losing the last of Will's money as Aggie and Will approached the ring toss game. The man in the booth looked up.

"Will Collins, my son!" the man exclaimed. "Well I'll be a...just the man I wants to see."

Will nodded his head curtly.

"Heber," he said. He didn't seem pleased. Aggie could see why. The man was unwashed and ill-shaven, and his clothes had seen better days. But Aggie disliked his eyes most — small, hard eyes that glittered when they latched on to Will.

"You knows this fellow, Will?" George asked.

"Oh, this youngster is a friend of yours, is he?" the man named Heber asked.

Will simply nodded his head.

"Friend?" George replied happily. "He's me brother."

The man behind the booth took this in greedily.

"Your brother then? All that time I sailed with you, Will Collins, you never spoke of no brother. I heard you'd come ashore." He turned to George and handed him an armful of rings. "Hear, try your luck again, my son. No charge. Any brother of Will Collins's is a friend to me." Then he fixed those hard eyes on Aggie. "Who's this then, your sister?"

Will moved closer to Aggie.

"No," he said, "She's not." He made no effort to introduce them.

"Heber Quigley, miss," the man said, "at your service."

"George," Will said, "we'll be going now."

"Not yet, Will, I'm just after warming up my arm."

"Take all the time you wants, my son," Heber said. "This is only a sideline for me, Will. I've a new boat in the harbour, just waiting for a crew. Could use a good hand like yourself. You in need of work these days?"

Will shook his head.

"Not with a rumrunner."

The older man looked around quickly to see if anyone had heard. Then he laughed weakly.

"Watch your language, Will. Not everyone would take that as a joke."

"Not everyone would..." Will started to say, but George interrupted.

"Three rings! I win."

"That you do, my son. And what'll it be?" Heber Quigley asked, pointing to the stuffed toys pegged to a line behind him.

"Aggie?" George asked.

Aggie pointed to a small brown teddy bear. The man took it down and held it out to her. "Aggie, is it? Some quiet for such a pretty maid. Likes a teddy bear, do you?" he asked.

"It's for her little sister," George said.

"We'll be going now, George," Will said. "Goodnight to you, Heber Quigley."

"Remember, Will, if you're looking for a berth on a vessel, I got one for you."

"Let's see that teddy bear, Aggie," George said as they walked away, "That fellow was some nice, Will."

"Nice is not a word I'd use in the same breath as Heber Quigley," Will said. "He's one reason why I came ashore. Heber Quigley's been running liquor across the lakes ever since Prohibition started. Almost went to jail once. When I met him, he'd lost his boat, was crewing on a laker. Kept saying he'd get another boat, kept after me to work for him. I suppose he finally got someone to bankroll him. I hate to think who."

"Is the pay any good?" George asked.

"Pay?" Will said. "Pay! George my son, working for a man like that, pay would be the least of your worries. Rum runners works for gangsters. You might land on the bottom of the lake. Heber Quigley is the worst sleeveen I ever laid eyes on."

"Still, he let me win the teddy bear for Aggie," George said. Only Aggie heard the sigh Will tried to suppress.

A few days later, Will came to call on Aggie in the evening. This was allowed now. When Mrs. Bradley realized that Aggie was seeing Will seriously, she'd spoken to Mrs. Stockwood.

"Many's the young domestic has come to harm for want of a place to entertain her suitor," she'd told Aggie. "A girl who can have a visitor in the kitchen is a sight safer."

Tonight, Will looked grim.

"George lost his job today," he said. "There was nothing I could do."

"Well, there must be plenty of jobs," Aggie said.

"Aggie maid, George is always up to mischief. When I'm there to keep an eye on him, I can keep him to his work. I thought perhaps I should leave this job as well."

"Will, no! You love working on that building," **Aggie** cried.

"So I do. But I feels responsible for George."

Aggie put her hand on Will's.

"I know you do, Will, but George canna expect you to follow him through life making things right, can he?"

Will shook his head. "I suppose not."

"Maybe you should let him fend for himself for a while," Aggie said. "He's no a bad lad, just feckless. It might do him some good to find his own way for a while."

"Perhaps you're right."

A few days later, Aggie had a letter from her mother, confirming the day and time in August when the family would arrive in Toronto. The handwriting was not as firm as usual, and letter ended: *Your new baby brother arrived a few days ago. He looked so like your brother that I could not help but call him Dougie. We will all be together soon.*

Dougie. Aggie sat silent for a moment, staring at the letter. They had called the new baby Dougie. People often called a child after a dead relative, but this seemed wrong to Aggie, as if it cancelled out her other brother's life. As if those twenty-one years meant nothing.

She went about her chores moodily that day, glad for once she wasn't seeing Will in the evening. That night, she dreamed herself back in Loughlinter, coming home from Mrs. MacDougall's house on the cobblestone street, and there was Dougie.

"Aggie, lass, did Mum tell you? I'm coming to Canada after all with the others," he said. But she could see, even as he spoke the words, that he didn't really believe them. And neither did she.

She thought about the dream when she woke. The new baby wasn't her Dougie and never could be. But now at least she felt she understood why her mother had given the child his name. It would ease the pain of leaving her older brother alone in that cold cemetery at the edge of Loughlinter.

On Sunday, when Aggie met Will, she told him about the new baby and her family's travel plans.

"So they're coming in August, are they?" Will said. "Should we start to look for a place?"

"Aye, I suppose so. At least that will give me an excuse to talk to Emma. I've hardly seen her since...since she told me about her trouble with Stuart." Aggie felt herself blushing, but Will only nodded tactfully. That made it easier. "Maybe I should pay more attention to her, Will. Perhaps she needs my help."

"Wouldn't Emma ask for your help if she needed it?"

"I'm not sure. With Emma I never know. In any case, I'll see if she wants to start looking for a house. Oh Will, I canna wait to see everyone again."

Will gave Aggie a serious look.

"I wonder what they'll think of me — your parents, I mean."

"My mum will like you, I'm sure, just as I do," she said quickly.

"And your father?" Will asked.

"My father...well, we'll have to see."

"Is he a hard case, your father?" Will asked. Aggie didn't like the anxious look in his eyes.

"I'm not sure what a hard case is, Will Collins," Aggie said, "not being from Newfoundland." When her joke didn't cheer him, she became serious. "My father likes things to be proper."

"And perhaps he won't find me proper enough for you."

Aggie had wondered this herself. She couldn't lie.

"You're not like the men he knows, Will. It's hard to explain. Perhaps he'll need time to get used to you. But dinna worry about that yet," she said. "Now, how are things with George?"

Will made a sour face.

"That's another story. Can't seem to find work, and worse, Heber Quigley has been talking to the boys at the boarding house, the old strife breeder. Putting ideas in their heads. A few of them might even crew for him. Now, George is no sailor, so I think he'll stay out of harm's way. At least I hope he will."

"How is he spending his time?" Aggie asked.

Will shrugged.

"Hanging around the boarding house mostly. I don't like it. He'll be out of money and into trouble shortly, I'm sure."

"He could come with us this Thursday," Aggie said. "It would give him something to do."

Will smiled. "You've a good heart, Aggie maid. Perhaps we'll take him to Sunnyside."

"But Will, I thought you'd want to keep him away from that Mr. Quigley."

"Don't worry. I hear Heber's moved on. I never knew him to stay with an honest job for long."

On Aggie's next half day, Will brought George and they went to Sunnyside. The park thronged with midsummer crowds now. There was no band concert on this night. The Auditorium Orthophonic Victrola blared "I Can't Give You Anything But Love" out over the soft night air. Aggie noticed something was different.

"There's more beach," she said to Will. "Look at the bandstand. Last summer it was at the end of a pier. Now it's at the water's edge."

Will nodded.

"I got some friends works on the stonehookers — the dredging boats. Harbour Commission's always on the go," he said. "Seems every time they get a bit of sand they rearrange the lakeshore."

Did anything stay the same in this country? Aggie wondered to herself. Nothing seemed to. Just last year, she thought, I walked this very boardwalk with Bobby Chandler. I thought a dance at the Palais Royale was the most important thing in the world. Now, the lakeshore has changed — and so have I.

As they walked on, men dressed as clowns passed out handbills to the crowd. Will took one and began to read it. Aggie noticed the frown on his face.

"What is it, Will?" she asked.

"Listen to this," and he read:

As a sacrifice to make a Roman holiday for the people whom she has carried across Toronto Bay for 50 years, the veteran ferry boat will disappear from the city's life, but not its memory as a great fiery spectacle on the lake. While scores of pretty girls in gay costumes dance, sing and toss confetti about and clowns make merry, an airplane will pour bombs into the John Hanlan and another yacht.

Will looked up. "It's set to go this Saturday at midnight."

"Oh, not the *Hanlan*!" Aggie cried. "That was the first ferry I ever took to the island."

"I knew they'd taken her out of service," Will said, "but I didn't expect this. I always liked the *Hanlan*, she was a fine old boat. You'd think they let a vessel rot away with dignity after all those years."

"Well, I think it's grand," George said.

Will gave him a withering look.

"And what would you know about ships?"

George blushed.

"Not much now, but I will. Just wait and see. A crowd of us is planning to sign on with Heber Quigley next week. He promised real good wages."

"That you will not, George my son." Will's voice was quiet but Aggie could hear his anger.

"Don't you 'my son' me, Will Collins. I'll do as I pleases. You're getting as bad as the old man, always telling me what to do."

Will grew pale.

"If either of us is like the old man, it's you. Spoilt young pup. I'm ashamed to have you for me brother. You will not set foot on that man's boat."

"See if you can stop me," George said, and he was gone.

Will would have gone after him, but Aggie put her hand on his arm.

"Give him time to calm down, Will," she said. "If you go after him now, you'll only fight."

"Perhaps you're right," Will said. They walked along the boardwalk a little farther, and there was the *Hanlan*, tied up against the breakwater, decked out in coloured pennants with the smaller yacht moored beside it. To Aggie, the *Hanlan* looked like something waiting to die.

"Oh, Will," she said, "This is so sad."

"That it is, Aggie, my maid," Will said. The evening was ruined. "No point in staying now," Will said after a few minutes. "I'll see you home."

Will sat silent on the streetcar, brooding. It wasn't until they stood outside the Stockwood house that Aggie tried to talk to him.

"Will," she said finally, "why would that man offer to take George on? You said yourself he's no a sailor."

"Heber Quigley is a shrewd old devil," Will said. "I've been thinking about it. I'm afraid he may be after me, using George as bait. You see, most of the men who sails these waters has only ever worked the larger vessels. Quigley needs someone who can navigate a small craft at night and in fog, someone who can out-manoeuvre larger vessels if needs be. I'm not bragging, Aggie maid, but I'm probably as good a hand with such a boat as anyone Heber's likely to know. And it didn't take him long to figure what George means to me."

Aggie's heart sank.

"Will, surely you'd not go and work for this man."

Will didn't reply right away.

"George is my family, Aggie — the only family I have. It's hard to say what he means to me. If he signs on with this man, his life may be in danger."

"But Will, you'd be giving up everything you've worked for here. Your life would be in danger too. You could go to jail." Tears sprang to her eyes. "Will, I couldn'a bear it. Please, tell me you'll no do this."

Will put his hands on her shoulders and looked into her eyes.

"Aggie, maid, I've got to do what's right. It's just that I haven't decided yet what that might be. We can talk again on Sunday. Perhaps by then I'll know."

Aggie couldn't stop the tears from falling. Will put his hand on her chin and wiped her cheek gently with his thumb.

"I never meant to cause you grief, Aggie. No matter what happens, you'll always know I never meant to hurt you." And then he was gone.

Aggie slept poorly that night. The next day she dragged herself through her chores. Mrs. Bradley noticed.

"Lovers' quarrel?" she asked Aggie in the afternoon.

"Not exactly," Aggie said. She felt she couldn't begin to explain.

"Well, I know it can seem like the end of the world, but whatever it is, these things have a way of working out," Mrs. Bradley said.

Aggie nodded. She appreciated Mrs. Bradley's kindness but was not convinced by her words. Sometimes things did not work out.

Will often stopped by on Friday nights to visit, but not this Friday. Saturday night came and went — and Will did not appear. This had never happened before. Lying in her bed late Saturday night, Aggie made up her mind to find Will on Sunday if he didn't come to see her. To find him and try to convince him that working for Heber Quigley could only be a terrible mistake. She lay awake most of the night, falling into a tense, dream-haunted sleep only after the first birds were singing in the trees outside.

In spite of Aggie's misgivings, Will appeared at the back door just after lunch on Sunday as usual. He was neatly dressed and freshly shaven, but he was pale and there were dark smudges under his eyes.

"Let's just walk to the park by the reservoir and sit," Will said. "I'm too tired to go any distance today."

"You look like you've hardly slept," Aggie said.

"I went to Sunnyside to see the *Hanlan* burn last night. To pay my respects, so to speak. The crowds were huge, more people than I'd ever seen in one place. I went a ways along the beach, away from the crowds so's I could see.

"It was a sight. There were boats on the water, with people throwing torches in to begin with. One fell back down and almost set a canoe on fire. Then the airplane came, and that's when she really went up. They'd set barrels of tar on her to make sure she burned. I don't imagine hell would burn any hotter than the *Hanlan* did last night. Looking at the crowds, the music, the fire on the lake...it was like looking into hell. It seemed as if it was my own past going up in smoke."

They came to the park now and found a bench. The bright summer sun shone through the trees all around them, but Aggie felt herself back in that dark night.

"The crowds started to thin out after a while," Will said, "and I went closer. By dawn, I was sitting right opposite the *Hanlan*, and she was nothing more than a pile of flankers smouldering on the water. All through the night I thought about my life on the water and my life on the land. I thought about my mother. She was a lovely, gentle woman, Aggie. I got neither photograph of her, but I remembers her face right well. I thought about George and what he aims to do. He's determined now. No amount of arguing will stop him.

"I thought about my future. By the time the sun hit my face, I knew what I wanted. Aggie, family is the most important thing to me, I think you knows as much."

Aggie nodded. She knew what Will was going to say. She was sure her heart would break.

"Family," Will said again and then he paused. "I got to thinking — a family is what I've been longing after. But perhaps I've been setting the wrong course. What I'm saying is, Aggie, it's time for me to think about my own family." He paused.

"So you're going to look after George," Aggie said. Her voice was flat. She stared at the ground without seeing anything. Will spoke with such determination, she was sure she could never change his mind.

Will ran his hand over his face.

"I'm tired," he said. "So perhaps I'm not speaking plainly. Aggie, the family I wants now is the one I make. It's only been three months and perhaps it's too soon, but I know my mind, if you do — Aggie, maid, I'm asking you to marry me."

At first Aggie thought she must be hearing things. Slowly she lifted her head and looked at Will. The anxious, questioning look on his face told her she had not heard wrong.

"If you'll have me," he added. He leaned towards her. They both seemed to have stopped breathing.

"It canna be soon, Will. You know that," Aggie said. "My family needs me still. Maybe you'll not want to wait so long."

"I've waited such a long time, maid. All my life, it seems. You're the only one I ever set my heart on. I'll wait for you as long as needs be."

Then Aggie threw her arms around Will's neck and kissed him as if there was no one else in the world.

Chapter Sixteen

A Tree Full of Butterflies

" 'Four bedroom house on St. Clair Avenue West, suit family,' it says. What do you know about St. Clair Avenue West?" Emma asked. They were sitting in a cafe, Aggie, Will and Emma, looking at the ads in the newspaper.

"Whereabouts?" Will asked. He placed his hand over Aggie's resting on the seat beside him and squeezed.

"It says at Keele."

"That's near to the stockyards," Will said.

Aggie wrinkled her nose.

"Will it no smell?"

"It may," Will said. "In that case the rent will be cheaper."

"I'll circle it," Emma said, and she read on. This was how Aggie spent her half days now, visiting likely houses, prowling through junk shops with Will and Emma. From comments her sister made, Aggie gathered that Emma was still seeing Stuart. But he never came with her and it was clear Emma didn't want to talk about him. Aggie knew there was no point in trying to make her.

The house on St. Clair faced the stockyards. The slaughter houses were right behind, and Aggie was right: the whole neighbourhood stank. But the house was big and well made and Will was right too: the rent was more than reasonable. So the two sisters put a deposit on the house and it was theirs from the beginning of August. To Aggie and Emma, the house seemed filthy. Determined to make it fit for their family, they attacked it on their half days with all energy and the skill of their combined years in domestic service.

Will helped with the heavy jobs and did whatever the girls asked. He had tried cleaning at first, but his work was quickly deemed inadequate, so mostly he looked on in wonder.

"I never knew two such enemies of dirt," he said one day, handing a bucket of clean, soapy water to Aggie. She was on her hands and knees, scrubbing the kitchen floor. The day was hot, and sweat trickled down her forehead.

"Cleanliness is next to godliness, Will. That's what our mum would say." Aggie said. She peered intently at the floor. "It's mostly built up wax, I think. We need steel wool."

"I could go look for some if you likes," Will offered. "I gets right uncomfortable, watching you two work so hard."

Aggie smiled.

"Will, my son, that would be grand."

Will laughed.

"We'll make a Newfoundlander of you yet, Aggie maid," and he was gone.

The two girls had worked without speaking for some time when Aggie heard a scrub brush fall. She glanced up to see Emma lurch a little, and put her hand up to her head.

"Emma! Are you all right?" Aggie crossed the slippery floor to her sister's side.

"Just a wee bit faint," Emma said. Her voice sounded as if it came from very far away. The colour had drained from her face.

"Well, let's get you off the kitchen floor. Oh, I wish there was a chair," Aggie glanced around the empty room. "Come into the hall." Aggie helped her sister into the hall and eased her onto the stairs. "Put your head down now, right between your knees. I'll get you a glass of cold water."

When Aggie returned with the water, Emma's head was up. Some of the colour was back in her face, but a tear trickled down her cheek. Aggie could not recall ever seeing Emma cry.

"Emma! Is something wrong?"

"I hope not, Aggie," Emma began, but the front door behind them swung open.

"Steel wool..." Will started to say. "What's wrong?"

"Emma nearly fainted."

"Must be the heat," Will said.

"Em, do you feel okay now?" Aggie asked. Emma nodded.

"Perhaps you'd like to go home, spend the rest of the day with your feet up," Will suggested.

"I think I will, Aggie, if you dinna mind being left with the work."

"Not at all, Em. Do you want us to go with you?"

"No, I'll be fine now, I'm sure," Emma said. She did look better, and she insisted on going home alone.

After she left, Will said, "We may as well bide here. Show me what to do with this steel wool. Perhaps I can be some help to you now."

Later, as they'd finished working, Aggie turned to Will.

"Emma's not herself these days. I've never seen her faint before. Do you think she could be sick?"

Will did not reply at first. Then he said softly,

O Rose, thou art sick
The invisible worm
That flies in the night,
In the howling storm,

Has found out thy bed
of crimson joy
and his dark secret love
Does thy life destroy.

He fell silent.

"Did you make that up?" Aggie asked.

"Me? No. My mother taught me that. It's by an English fellow, William Blake. Had some strange ideas, Blake did, but he was a fine hand with a poem."

"But Will, what does it mean?" Aggie asked.

"Nothing, I hope," Will said quietly. "I just thought of it now is all. Well, at least we got the floor clean. I'll take you somewheres for supper."

"Let me wash up then."

After they'd washed, Aggie tidied the sink. Will came up behind her and began to unpin her hair. Aggie laughed. "Will, what are you doing?"

"Shh," he said. He combed out her hair with his fingers. Then he wrapped his arms around her waist and buried his face in her hair. Aggie relaxed against him. All the tiredness and worry drained from her body. They stood together like that, not moving, for a long moment. Aggie closed her eyes. I'd be happy to stay like this forever, she thought.

"Aggie," Will said at last, "I don't suppose your parents have had time to write you about our news, have they?"

Aggie tensed and pulled away, suddenly embarrassed. She kept her head down, busying herself with the kitchen sink again.

"Aggie, you did write to tell them, didn't you?"

Aggie turned to face him. She shook her head.

"They've so much to think about just now Will. The new baby, coming to Canada...I thought I'd wait until they're here."

The disappointment in his eyes was almost more than she could bear.

"Are you ashamed of me?" he asked quietly.

"No! Will. How could you think such a thing? It's just...my father. I've never been able to stand up to him. I'm sure he thinks I'll ask for his approval before I marry anyone. I didn'a want him to come here angry to begin with, angry with you."

Will stood silent for a long moment, then said, "Aggie, why don't we get married now?"

"Now?"

"Yes. In the next few weeks I mean. If we're married, there won't be anything they can do. They'll have to accept it. We could find ourselves a little place like this..."

Aggie's nose wrinkled.

"...well, not like this exactly, but a place of our own. We could be together. You wouldn't have to clean other people's houses. I don't like to see you slave like this."

"Will, I canna do that. You know why."

"Aggie, I've got money put by. I could help your family."

Aggie shook her head.

"My father would never hear of it, Will. You'll understand after you've met him. He's too proud to take your money."

"I've never laid eyes on this man, and I'm after disliking him already."

"Will, dinna say that."

"Just promise me you'll think about marrying me now?"

Aggie hesitated.

"If you want me to," she said finally. "But I'll need some time to think. Give me a week."

"You want to go a week without seeing me?" he asked. They had never spent more than a few days apart since the night they met on the ferry.

"Will, if I'm to make the right choice, I need some time alone. If I'm with you, it's too easy to say yes. You remember, when you were trying to make up your mind about George, you took a few days to yourself."

Will nodded.

"So I did. Well, a week then. Let's say I'll see you a week from today."

"Thank you, Will," Aggie said. She reached up and kissed him. "Now, what about dinner?"

For the first few days, Aggie tried not to think at all. She wanted to let the feeling of being with Will wear off so she could think more clearly. But when Sunday came, she missed Will so much she could barely stop herself from going out to look for him. What I need, she thought, is someone to talk to. But who? Emma is too wrapped up in her own troubles just now. If only Mum were here, she thought.

Who else could she talk to? Hannah. Hannah would know what to do, Aggie was sure. She flew out the door and down to the streetcar stop, without thinking about what she was doing. She was on the Spadina streetcar before it occurred to her to wonder if Moshe Mendorfsky would welcome her. But it was too late to stop. If Aggie didn't go to the Mendorfskys, she would surely stay on the streetcar until she came to King Street, too near the cafe where Will was almost certain to eat his dinner. She knew she could not come looking for him four days early without also saying she would marry him as soon as he wanted. I'll stay in the kitchen, Aggie thought. Rachel and Moshe won't need to know I'm there. She got off the streetcar and retraced the path she had first taken with Hannah all those months before.

When the Mendorfskys' kitchen door opened, Aggie found herself enveloped in a warm hug. Then Hannah stood her at arm's length.

"So beautiful you are looking, Agnes. You must be in love," Hannah said. "Yes?"

Aggie nodded shyly.

"Rachel and Moshe are in parlour," Hannah said. "You go in, surprise Rachel. She has missed you."

Aggie's heart leapt into her throat.

"Oh, Hannah, I dinna think..."

But Hannah would not listen.

"Come," she said, and took Aggie by the hand.

Rachel was sitting on the sofa with Moshe, reading a book.

"Did you bring lemonade, Hannah?" she asked and then she looked up. "Agnes!" she cried, and rose to meet her friend. Aggie noticed the thickness in Rachel's waist right away. Rachel followed her gaze and laughed. "I am getting fat, yes?" she said, putting her hands over her waist. "The doctor says baby will be born in January." She beamed.

"Oh Rachel, I'm so happy for you."

"Yes, we are happy too," Moshe said. Even he seemed pleased to see Aggie.

"Come, sit beside me," Rachel said. "So often I think about you. Hannah, will you bring lemonade now?"

Aggie told Rachel of her family, her new baby brother, and the house on St. Clair Avenue. Rachel listened attentively.

"So now, everything is happy in your life, yes?" Rachel said.

"Yes," Aggie said, not without reluctance. Rachel gave her a questioning look. When it was time to go, Rachel walked out into the hall and hugged Aggie.

"Now you talk with Hannah," Rachel whispered quickly. "Hannah is wise. If you have trouble, you tell to her." Then she said more loudly, "One day you come back to visit on Thursday afternoon. We will talk like before."

Aggie went into the kitchen.

"You eat dinner?" Hannah asked.

"Hannah, it's three in the afternoon," Aggie said.

"So you have another glass of lemonade and talk to me."

It was easy to feel comfortable with Hannah. Aggie quickly told her everything about her family and Will.

"So he wants me to marry him now," she finished, "before they come. I don't know what I should do."

"This man, do you love him?" Hannah asked.

"So much, sometimes it seems as if we are one person in two bodies."

Hannah nodded.

"This is love," she said. "But when you are married it is forever. It is not good to hurry forever."

"But my father..." Aggie said.

"Why your family is coming to Canada, Agnes?" Hannah asked.

"To get away from the mines, of course," Aggie said, but Hannah swept this reply aside.

"No. This is not what I am asking. Your family is coming to Canada because you work so hard. Because you make...what is word? Sacrifice. All winter, I am thinking no daughter ever works so hard for her family. You know you love this man. You must tell your father you have earned the right to make your marriage. And he must listen. This is new land. In new land there are new ways," Hannah spoke with determination. "And then you will marry when you are ready. Not to fool parents. Not as if your love is shameful thing. You will have proper wedding, under canopy with all your family. Not under canopy," she amended, "But with all your family to share your joy and wish you happy life." Aggie sat quietly for a while, thinking about what Hannah had said.

"You're right," she said at last. "I've been so confused, trying to decide. But everything you said is exactly right."

Hannah smiled. "When you are old woman like me, it is easy to be right. Agnes, you always have lived to please other people. Now is your time to please you. Do what is best for you."

When she left the Mendorfsky house, Hannah hugged her again.

"You come back, tell me how story ends," she said.

"I will," Aggie promised. "Rachel asked me to as well."

On the streetcar, Aggie thought about what Hannah had said. She felt she had spent the last few days in a cage. Now, Hannah had unlocked it for her.

On Thursday, when Will came, he did not ask Aggie for her answer right away. Instead, he asked her to go to the island.

"Been working non-stop, Aggie maid," he said. "That house is almost perfect and you need a day off." When they boarded the streetcar, Will said, "Heber Quigley let George go. Even bootleggers needs hard workers it seems."

"Oh Will, I'm so pleased."

"Yes, I figure now, if I'd've gone after George we'd probably both be working for that old devil still. George came to me, asking for help to find a proper job again. Seems like he's had some of the wind knocked out of his sails. The whole thing might have done him some good."

"Well, I hope so."

"And how's Emma?" Will asked.

"I haven't seen her since last week. Will, I hope Emma is all right."

Will looked at Aggie seriously for a moment before he spoke.

"It may be that Emma's headed for trouble, Aggie. That Stuart Donaldson sounds like a bad one. But she's your sister and that makes her part of my crowd now. No matter what happens, we'll look out for her." He spoke with such fervour that Aggie felt better.

"Well, I hope she stays away from the house today. There's not much left to do now."

"I got the loan of a truck next Thursday evening if you wants it." Will said, "We could pick up the furniture you got deposits on, get most of it into the house."

"That would be wonderful."

The day was bright and cloudless, but not too hot — one of those August days when everything suddenly seems clear and sharply defined after the haze of summer. When they reached the ferry docks Will said, "We'll go to Ward's Island today." Aggie wondered why. There was nothing on Ward's but places where people camped in the summertime.

Will hardly spoke, but Aggie could see how anxious he was. After they boarded the ferry, Aggie could hardly stand the tension.

"Will," she said, "We need to talk."

"Not yet, Aggie. There's something I want to show you first, if it's still there."

When they got off the ferry, Will only said, "This way." He guided her past the funny little houses with their wooden walls and canvas roofs, towards the Eastern Gap. Here they came to a few big willow trees that stood alone on a grassy field.

"Keep your eyes down till I tells you," Will said, leading her towards one of the trees. "Now, look up."

Aggie looked up and caught her breath. The tree was covered with hundreds, maybe thousands, of orange butterflies, their bright wings splashed with black and white, glowing in the sunshine. The whole tree looked like some kind of flower. Sometimes a gentle breeze blew a cloud of butterflies off a branch. They drifted against the blue sky for a moment, then slowly fluttered back. Aggie and Will stood beneath the tree for a long time, speechless.

"I've never seen anything like it," Aggie said at last. "It's beautiful."

"I was out here yesterday. I just hoped they'd still be here." Will said. "Monarchs they're called. Never seen them 'til I came to Ontario."

"But why are they here?" Aggie asked. "Do you know?"

"Waiting to fly south, I believe."

"You're joking!"

"No maid, I'm telling you the truth. And now perhaps you'll do the same for me. Aggie, I needs to know."

Aggie turned to face him.

"I'll marry you, Will Collins," she said. "Never doubt that. But I want a proper wedding, as a friend of mine would say, with all my family to share our joy and wish us a happy life."

"And your father?"

"He'll have to understand," Aggie said. She wished she felt as certain as she sounded.

"I've had a week to think myself," Will said. He paused. "Aggie, there only ever was my mother and myself. You knows as much. I can't lie to you, my maid. The idea of sharing you with so many people scares me. I panicked, I suppose. But it would be wrong for me to force a wedge between you and your family. I knows nothing about being part of a family such as yours. But if you stand beside me, I'm willing to learn."

"I'll stand beside you, Will."

Will smiled.

"I had time to do a bit of shopping last week when I was on my own. I never bought one of these before, so perhaps it won't be to your liking, but I wondered if you might wear it, as a token."

He drew a small box from his jacket pocket and opened it. Inside was a narrow gold band with a tiny diamond and two small rubies.

"I've never seen anything as lovely," she said.

"Then perhaps you'll let me put it on your hand." Will drew the ring out of the box and took her left hand. Above them, a tree full of butterflies fluttered against the bright blue sky.

The night before her family was to arrive in Toronto, Aggie dreamed herself back in Loughlinter. She was standing by the iron gate of the cemetery in a winter drizzle. Behind her, she knew, was the automobile that would carry her to Glasgow and the ship. She passed old stone markers etched with lichen and found the unmarked grave where her brother lay.

"Goodbye, Dougie," she said softly. "I'm leaving for Canada now." And she turned away. When she reached the cemetery gate, she saw the borrowed auto. But Will, not her father, stood waiting for her.

"Come along, Aggie maid," he said, putting his arm around her. "They expect you to meet them at the station."

When Aggie woke, the house was dark and quiet. Only a few hours and her family would be here. She held on to the dream for a moment. Wherever her brother Dougie was now, she felt sure he was not beneath the cold, hard ground outside Loughlinter. She rose and dressed quietly and slipped down to the kitchen to eat breakfast. To her surprise, a box was waiting on the kitchen table with her name on it. Inside she found soft, thick towels, the colour of daffodils and a note: *A present for your family, with best wishes, Mr. and Mrs. Stockwood.*

While she ate, Aggie studied the ring winking on her finger. The thought of facing her father gave her butterflies. Then she remembered the tree full of butterflies, and the look in Will's eyes when he'd placed this ring on her finger. She took a deep breath. She hoped her father would take to Will. Perhaps he wouldn't. Will came to the kitchen door a few minutes later and they set off together while the sun came up casting long, rosy shadows on the new day.

Union Station was as quiet and cathedral-like as it had been that winter day a year and a half before when Aggie came in from the train alone. Emma was waiting for them. Aggie tried to read her face. She thought she saw a new sadness in her sister's eyes. But then people began to come in from the tracks and there was no time to think what that might mean. For suddenly, there was Callum, looking so out of place in his short pants, then Ewan and James and Flora and Jen. Emma and Aggie bounded away from Will. Could that be Jen? She was so tall! Then Jen flew into Aggie's arms. They hugged and Aggie knew this big girl really was her little sister. When Aggie looked up again, her mother and father were there.

The baby called Dougie was asleep in her mother's arms. Aggie went to her mother and kissed her.

"He must be heavy, Mum," she said. "Let me take him for you." As Aggie reached for the baby, her mother noticed the engagement ring. A look of surprise crossed her face, but she said nothing as she gave the baby to Aggie. The weight of him pressed against Aggie's heart. As soon as she touched him, she forgave him for taking her brother's name. Then she looked up and saw Will watching her, standing awkward and alone by the bench where she'd left him.

Aggie glanced at her parents. Her father had noticed Will. He looked at Aggie and raised his eyebrows.

"That lad over there is watching you, Aggie," he said. "Do you know him?"

Aggie met her father's eyes without flinching.

"That I do, Da. He came here to meet you, to meet you all." Then, suddenly, Aggie knew she was not afraid of her father. She was not the girl he'd left at the docks in Glasgow all those months before. This had nothing to do with Will. For the first time, Aggie realized how strong she could be.

She went to Will, her small brother still in her arms.

"Have you ever held a baby?" she asked. He shook his head. "After you've met everyone, I'll show you how." She smiled up at him. "Someday you'll need to know."

He put his arm around her shoulder and she took him to meet her family.

Historical Note

My mother's three sisters, Jean, Barbara, and Janet McIvor, came to Toronto as teenagers in 1927 and 1928 to work as domestic servants. In October of 1929 the rest of the McIvor family followed, including my mother Isabel, who was eight. This book is not their story, but knowing about the experiences of my mother's sisters helped me to create Aggie and to understand what her life might have been like.

In the 1920s, Canadians did not yet understand that people from many different parts of the world could enrich this country and make it a better place. Immigration of those who seemed different from Anglo-Canadians was discouraged. This is why Rachel had to enter Canada as a sponsored domestic servant. Like Emma, most people were not tolerant of cultural differences. They believed that immigrants should become like Anglo-Canadians as quickly as possible.

People had different ideas about social class in those days too. A girl like Aggie could not expect to have friends who were richer or more educated than she was. There was little hope that she could get an education or even marry above her own social class.

The "Roaring Twenties" was a decade of growth and money. Airplanes carried mail for the first time, and more women entered Canadian universities than ever before. All this changed in October of 1929, when a crash on the New York stock market signalled the beginning of the Great Depression, which lasted through the 1930s. Today, the Palais Royale, the bathing pavilion, and the children's wading pool are the only reminders of Toronto's Sunnyside Amusement Park, which was gradually torn down in the 1950s.

But in the 1920s no one could foresee that future. In 1928 and 1929, Toronto was an exciting place, full of beautiful new buildings and dazzling amusement parks. Flappers with bobbed hair and short dresses danced at the Palais Royale, and it seemed as if the party would go on forever.

(Note: Och is a Scottish exclamation. It is pronounced with a hard K sound, something like ock.)